The Witch's Chair
Book One in the Gifted Series.

Emma Sharp

Copyright © 2024 Emma Sharp

All rights reserved.

ISBN: 9798322522058

DEDICATION

To my editor, my mentor and my friend, Russell.

Other books by Emma Sharp

The World Beyond – Gifted book 2

The Letter – Chateau trilogy book 1

Sweet Pea – Chateau trilogy book 2

Secrets and Surprises – Chateau trilogy book 3

Innocence in Provence – book 1 of the Carboni family saga.

The Lemon Tree – book 2 of the Carboni family saga.

Tea and Cake – a short story

Web - www.emma-sharp-author.com

Email - info@emma-sharp-author.com

ACKNOWLEDGMENTS

Cover design by Sarah Jane Design

Edited by Russell Gregory

1.

"Alan..."

Alan looked up from his gadget and sighed; pushing his glasses back up his nose he braced himself. He knew by the tone of Rose's voice that she was hatching a plan. "Mm...," he responded, knowing full well that, after recently purchasing his third Alfa Romeo, he wasn't in a position to negotiate.

"Our things look so out of place in this cosy, old cottage."

"And...?"

"Well, I was just thinking – perhaps we ought to buy a few antiques?"

Realising it was a rhetorical question, he knew there was no point in challenging his wife. She was, after all, right on this occasion. The oversized modern clock taking up most of the wall in the lounge looked ridiculous. It had fitted the décor so well in their previous home. In fact, he remembered, that was one of the reasons they'd bought it, to dress the house up to sell. It had worked too.

Leaning back in his chair, he smiled at his wife. "What had you got in mind exactly?"

"Well, there's an antiques fair at Ripley Castle next weekend, I saw it on the internet, and I thought..."

"But I've got an event next weekend, I can't go..." Noting the look on her face he paused, knowing full well that many weekends were rather dominated by his motor sport events and she was generally good natured about it, usually finding ways to keep herself occupied. "Why don't you see if one of the girls would like to go with you. Anyway, I wouldn't be much use - I'm clueless when it comes to antiques, unless of course they've got four wheels."

Disappointed once more, she lowered her gaze back down and sighed; she was beyond fed-up of playing second fiddle to his beloved cars. Closing her eyes, she tried to cast her mind back over the last few years and quickly came to the conclusion that he was indeed getting worse. It was almost an obsession now – everything revolved around cars and his motor sport events. He showed little interest in her hobbies and even laughed when she'd suggested he accompany her to a healing fair a few months ago. But she went on her own anyway and had a super time – so much so that a few weeks ago she had at last taken the plunge and secretly joined a local spiritual circle of eclectic witches. Not quite knowing what to expect she'd been pleasantly surprised. There had been no animal sacrifices or dancing naked amongst the trees; just down to earth, friendly people who wanted to support each other and live sustainably. Of course, there was no point telling him, she mused. No, he would most likely poke fun at her, and he hadn't even noticed the bunches of herbs hung high in the rafters of the kitchen ceiling, or the crystal ball carefully placed on the bedroom window sill where it could bathe in the light of the full moon. She'd had enough of his selfishness. Now she had a new circle of like-minded friends, nothing like the petrol heads and their wives that he hung around with, who were only adding to the climate crisis.

Later that evening, Rose was thrilled. Their eldest daughter Amy, had agreed to go with her to the antiques fair. Amy had always been interested in vintage items, mainly retro stuff from the sixties and seventies; she often picked them up for peanuts in charity shops. But Rose was looking for older pieces. Much older pieces.

Having driven over the night before to spend the weekend with her mum, Amy and Rose were up with the larks eager to visit their first antique fair. Finding a parking space was challenging but soon they'd paid their eight pounds entry fee and found themselves surrounded by stalls. Some were simple trestle tables adorned with bric-a-brac, others were sophisticated, tented structures housing elaborate pieces of furniture. Rose found herself wondering how on earth they'd managed to get such large items there, and, if she were to buy anything, how she'd get it home?

"So Mum, just what had you got in mind?"

Looking about her, Rose shrugged feeling somewhat out of her depth. "I'm not sure. I want things that will fit in – you know, the right dates for the cottage. Period items."

She let her eyes wander and take in the scene, gradually becoming more confident, certain that she would know when she found the right pieces.

Breaking into her thoughts, Amy put her hand on her shoulder. "Okay, when was the cottage built?"

"Well, I've traced the original building back as far as 1854, but it's had several extensions added over the years."

Frowning, Amy got her phone out and consulted her favourite search engine while Rose, trance-like, imagined life back then; no mobile phones, no internet. The house probably didn't have any facilities at all when it was first built; no electricity, and the toilet would have been a hole in the garden.

Tucking her phone back into her bag, Amy smiled. "So, we're looking at Victorian, Edwardian and Art Deco. Plenty to choose from."

Linking arms, the pair strode off purposefully, stopping to pick up items of interest. It soon became obvious that Rose was particularly drawn to the wooden pieces. A pair of unusual, candlesticks caught her attention. Touching them, she looked at the vendor. "What can you tell me about these?"

"Beauties, aren't they?"

But Rose couldn't answer. She felt herself being transported to another dimension. All she could see was a blinding white landscape. She began to shiver. Nothing made sense anymore.

"Spalted maple. They're old."

Jolted back to the present, she stared at the objects in her hands.

"Exactly how old?" It was Amy this time, questioning the old man.

"Erm – can't tell you exactly, but they've got a great patina…"

"I'll give you twenty-five."

Stunned, Rose looked at her poker-faced daughter, wondering just when she'd become so savvy.

The old man sucked in his ruddy cheeks and let out a long breath. "For you pretty lady I can do forty."

Continuing her charade, Amy took the candlesticks out of her mother's hands and swiftly placed them back on the stall. "Come on Mum, we've only just arrived. There's masses more to see."

As Amy stepped away, ushering her bemused mother in

front of her, the old man continued, "Thirty-five and they're yours."

Briefly turning her head, feigning disinterest, Amy responded, "You can't even tell me their age. Last chance, twenty-five."

Amy almost missed his imperceptible nod.

"Okay, deal."

Once wrapped in newspaper, she handed them to Rose who was somewhat bewildered. "Here you are Mum, a housewarming gift."

Thrilled, Rose stood on her toes and gave Amy a peck on her cheek. "Thanks, Love."

The next item they acquired was a tall, salt glazed, German vase from the sixties that Amy persuaded her Mum to purchase, and Rose knew exactly which window sill she wanted to place it on.

An hour later and they were three quarters of the way around the fair but still hadn't bought much. Rose had been drawn to several exquisite mantle clocks, but they were well outside of her budget.

The afternoon clouds grew darker and darker, chasing away the late summer sunshine and Rose noticed some of the traders were packing up. "It's going to pour down, perhaps we should go, Love."

"No Mum, now's the chance to grab a bargain."

"But, Amy, our coats are in the car!"

"So, we'll get wet – you won't go rusty Mum."

As if on cue the heavens opened and Rose dragged Amy under the awning of a large motorhome, where the owner was frantically stashing his hoard back inside his van. The man grinned at the two women seeking shelter from the storm and continued with his task, picking up a heavy clock.

"Stop!" Rose shouted, louder than she'd intended. "Can I see that?"

Eagerly, she took it from his outstretched hands feeling the solid weight of the piece. Turning it over she noticed the steep price tag and hesitated, but she knew she had to have it when strange tingling feelings began traveling up her arms. It was as if the clock was trying to tell her something.

Astutely, Amy took it from her. Was there a deal to be done? She knew her mother had set her heart on a chiming, mantle clock. The ones she'd been looking at were too frilly and showy – very feminine, but this one was different. It was simple, solid but elegant, almost masculine. It commanded your attention in a serious sort of way and was larger too. It would look perfect on the oak mantle above the woodburning stove.

Looking over to Amy, Rose found her voice. "What can you tell me about the clock?"

The man stopped his task and cupped his ears to indicate he couldn't hear her very well with the fat rain drops now crashing into the overhead awning, threatening to overwhelm him.

This time, shouting as loud as her vocal cords would allow, she tried again. "The clock! What can you tell me about it?"

Standing upright and running his hand through his damp hair he smiled. He could smell a sale. It had been a quiet day and he'd hardly made enough money to cover his expenses. And now it was chucking it down!

"I'm asking three hundred, but you can have it for two-fifty."

Again, Amy stepped in. "Does it work?"

The man set the clock on its base, opened the back, and attached the polished, star-shaped brass pendulum, setting it in motion.

"Would you guarantee it? When was it last serviced?"

Shrugging, the man turned to Rose, sensing a softer personality, "It's Edwardian, from about nineteen-ten."

Rose's heart skipped; it was exactly what she wanted. "Does it chime?" she enquired with anticipation, now oblivious to the sound of the summer storm drowning out all other signs of life around them. It was as if they were in their own mini time capsule.

Obligingly, the optimistic vendor wound the hand around to the hour and, sure enough, the clock gave out a series of resounding bongs. Four of them to be precise. Rose had counted every one and was now beaming at Amy.

Sighing, Amy shook her head. "Come on Mum, it's over budget; there's another fair at Thirsk in a couple of weeks."

Disappointed and annoyed, Rose stared back at her daughter about to contradict her. It was, after all, her money, not Amy's.

"Two-two-five," the vendor added, sensing his sale slipping away.

"Two hundred, that's our limit. Come on Mum."

Amy put her hand on her mother's shoulder and gave it a gentle squeeze before turning away.

"Deal."

Shocked, Rose turned. "What?"

His voice was quieter now, as though he wasn't quite sure he agreed it himself. "You can have it for two hundred. Cash." Scrabbling for her purse Rose hurriedly counted out the notes and took possession of the precious clock, now nestled in her embrace. Thrilled, Rose and Amy drove home, soggy but excited. By the time they reached their cosy, old cottage the clock had a name. Edward.

2.

After examining her new purchases, Rose carefully placed Edward on the oak mantle. Both women stood back in admiration. He looked stunning. They both agreed it was exactly what the old room needed. Contented, they shared a meal and a bottle of red, watched a film then bid each other goodnight. Rose climbed into bed with a warm glow in her heart, happy and secure in the knowledge that Amy was a short way down the corridor; she was asleep the moment her head hit the pillow.

Waking with a jolt, Rose sat up in bed and listened. What was that? The memories of the previous day flooded back, and she relaxed. It was Edward. It must be midnight. She smiled to herself and laid back, remembering the information Amy had unearthed on the internet; she had found the maker's mark inside the old clock which told them he had indeed been fabricated in nineteen-ten, but he wasn't British. No, he'd been made in Germany, Berlin to be precise. Yawning, Rose was soon asleep again; half a bottle of Malbec had taken its toll, causing her to have a vivid dream.

"Ester, take Frieda and go down the street to the Schmidt's family, they have a void under their floor – they will hide you."

Horrified, Ester stared at her husband, Joseph. She couldn't possibly abandon him to deal with the enemy alone; they weren't known for their compassion. "I'm not leaving you!"

Josephs words became harsh, broken, his eyes wide with fear. He knew this day would come and he had prepared. "Just go!" he shouted, pushing his wife and daughter out into the cold, dark street, handing her a black shawl, Frieda's red beret and her favourite teddy bear that he'd bought her for her birthday. He took one last look at his beautiful family before closing and locking the door behind them, knowing he might well never see them again, but he had to try and save his business from being destroyed by the Nazis. He was a clockmaker, as was his Father, and Grandfather before him. He was determined that everything they had worked for would one day be handed down to Frieda and the baby now growing inside Ester.

Terrified, Ester wrapped the handmade shawl around her beautiful daughter, placed her beret on her head and bundled her down the side of the shop into the back yard. Stumbling, they took the dark rear passage between more houses and businesses until they reached the door of their good friends, Karl and Ingrid Schmidt.

Ingrid welcomed the sobbing couple while Karl swiftly moved a heavy table to one side, lifted the carpet, and once more they were bundled down a makeshift ladder into a small void with barely enough height to stand.

Karl tugged at a board in the wall which eventually yielded, then guided mother and daughter into a tiny room. The board was quickly secured behind them, and they were left in the dark. By now Frieda was inconsolable, the small teddy bear that she was hugging offering her little comfort. Ester managed to settle her daughter on the blankets and cushions that had been placed on the floor, whispering stories of happier times into her ear.

Once the child was asleep, Esther rummaged about in the dark and found a small torch; it gave off a dim light, but it was enough to appraise her surroundings. There was a crate in the corner containing food and cans of water. The opposite corner housed a porcelain chamber pot. How long were they to stay down here? What would become of Joseph, her poor, brave husband? And the Schmidts? If they were caught harbouring Jews, they would be tortured and shot!

Waking with a jolt, she could hear harsh voices and banging doors above her. Was it the Nazis? Was this the end for her, Frieda, and their unborn child? Trying to quell the nausea deep within, she held tight to her daughter and prayed. What was to become of them?

Esther had lost all sense of time; how long had she and Freida been incarcerated under the floor? Had the noise above been merely hours, or days ago? She was desperate to hear any news about her dearest husband. Had the Nazis spared him? A scraping noise above them woke Frieda who was fretful. Ester tried to comfort her daughter who grew more fearful when they heard footsteps coming down the ladder. The loose board in the wall was quickly removed to reveal Karl staring into the void.

Sagging with relief, Ester reached out to him. "Have you seen Joseph?" Karl tried to hide his face, but Esther could sense his despair. "Tell me! What's happened? Have they taken him?"

This was the moment Karl had dreaded the most when he'd made hasty plans with his good friend Joseph. Both he and Joseph knew the risks they were taking, Joseph paying the ultimate price for the safety of his family. The Nazis had been and searched Karl and Ingrid's dwelling and business premises but thankfully, they were unable to find any Jews. Karl feared they would be back and knew Ester and Freida were in great danger until they managed to get them over the border. Ingrid was discreetly working with other sympathisers in the area to help them, but Karl had the unenviable task of telling Ester that Joseph had been taken and their shop looted. All that he'd been able to find were a few personal effects and an old clock that had been well hidden, probably the work of Josephs' late father.

Sobs wracked Esters body. How could one person have so much hatred that they could influence others to cause such harm to fellow humans?

At 5am, Edward's resounding chimes woke Rose. Her damp hair was plastered to her forehead, and she had a throbbing head. Feeling a bit spaced out, she made her way to the kitchen for a drink.

3.

Unable to return to her bed, Rose sat in the lofty kitchen under the drying herbs drinking strong black coffee. Was it the wine or her newfound interest that had induced the dream, or both perhaps? Either way, she was desperate to know what had happened to poor Joseph and his family. How could she return? Restless, she roamed around the cottage as the dawn broke, sending shards of glittering sunlight through the patio doors into the airy dining room. This was Rose's favourite room; for some reason she felt drawn to it. The light, in the height of summer gave it magical qualities. Perhaps she could set up her altar in here. It didn't need to be an elaborate affair, just a small space to place a few candles and crystals with some dried herbs. Alan wouldn't even notice; he'd think it was potpourri. Anyway, he was either at work, in his garage, or attending some motor sport event. It deeply saddened Rose when she realised that they now lived separate lives. An uneasy sensation took root deep in her gut when a nagging doubt entered her head. Was he really going to a motor sport event, or did he have someone else on the side? He wouldn't, would he? Not her Alan!

"Morning. Did you sleep well?" It was Amy breaking into her unpleasant thoughts, still in her pyjamas, hugging a mug of tea.

Standing on her tiptoes Rose gave her daughter a peck on the cheek. "Morning darling, how are you?"

Amy looked at her phone. "Fine, but sorry, I've got to dash after breakfast, Mum. I promised Tom I'd help him today."

Knowingly, Rose smiled, aware it was code for, *I've done my bit for mum and now it's time to get out of here.* But she didn't mind; today she needed space. And she didn't ever want to become a burden to their two beautiful daughters. Alan wouldn't be back until late, and today Rose wanted to practise her newfound witchcraft.

Once the breakfast dishes were tidied away and Amy had left, she locked the doors, took several deep breaths, trying to dispel unpleasant thoughts of Alan, then placed beeswax candles in her new spalted maple candlesticks. Next, Rose consulted her recently purchased book of hedge witch herbal spells then set up her small altar on the sideboard in the dining room with the required materials. It was time. She was determined to travel back, to find out what had happened to poor Joseph and his family.

Carefully following the instructions, Rose took sips of the mugwort tea as she gazed at the smoke curling from the burning incense sticks, filling the air with a heady aroma. She tried to picture images of the terrified family fleeing into the night as she quietly chanted 'mote it be'.

Frustratingly, an hour later, nothing had come to her. Perhaps she was trying too hard. Feeling defeated, she tidied her things away and took the dog out for a long walk in the adjacent countryside. That always lifted her spirits.

It was dark when Alan returned. He gave her a peck on the cheek and patted her bottom. It had always irritated her when he did that; it felt patronising, condescending even. Her inner goddess was urging her to respond with a knee to his testicles, but propriety overcame her, so she bit her tongue and put the kettle on like the dutiful wife that she'd been for nearly thirty-seven years.

"Have you had a good weekend?" she asked, secretly beginning to wonder if he indeed had a mistress. Could that be the real reason he spent so much time away?

After telling her in great detail about the tests and regularities he'd navigated, he turned the television on and found this weekend's Grand Prix race, then zoned out. Soon after, Edward struck ten o clock and Alan didn't even raise an eyebrow. Disappointed, Rose retreated to the dining room with a glass of red wine and sat with her laptop, annoyed that he hadn't even got the good grace to ask her about her weekend with Amy.

Glancing over to her new altar she smiled, if he hadn't noticed Edward then he wouldn't notice the bowl of crushed herbs and her beautiful candlesticks. Spalted maple, that's what the man had said. Picking them up she examined the base. There was a faded mark on one that she hadn't noticed earlier. Finding her glasses, she put the central light on and squinted. Ontario. One word. Running her fingers over the smooth surface she smiled. They were from Canada. They must be made from Canadian maple. But how old were they? An internet search came up with no answers for her, so she went to bed.

An hour or so later Rose woke to loud snoring. Alan had come to bed. Twenty minutes later she began to get annoyed; even her earplugs couldn't block out the dreadful sound. Enough was enough. Slipping her feet into her mules, she padded along the corridor to the spare room and climbed into the freshly made bed where she sank into a deep sleep.

It was cold, icy cold, and it would be dark soon. Where was John? Alice was beginning to get concerned. She turned to her youngest son, David. "Did you see John down by the lake?"

"Yes, he was skating with Mary, I don't know what the attraction is."

Jack smiled, remembering back to his youth. He leaned over and ruffled David's hair. "He's in love. You'll understand when you're a bit older, son."

"Yuk!" the twelve-year-old replied, gluing another piece

onto his model spitfire, just like the one his father had flown during the war.

The door to their wooden cabin burst open causing a draught which fanned the flames of the fire in the hearth. All heads turned to see Grace, a neighbour, standing in the doorway, looking as ashen as the leaden clouds above.

Alice was startled, "What is it, Grace?" closing the distance to her lifelong friend.

Grace stood rooted to the spot, unable to say the words forming on her lips. How could she tell them? It would shatter their lives.

Albert appeared behind his wife, his face sombre. "Get your coat Jack."

Alice hastily reached for her black coat and scarf hung behind the door, fearing the worst. "What is it, Albert?"

Albert nodded towards David. "Stay here with the boy."

Jack stared at his wife, silently warning her to take the advice, then hurried out of the door with Albert, leaving the two women behind with David."

Hurrying through the deep snow, the two men ploughed on in silence, stopping only to catch their breath. Jack couldn't bring himself to ask; he already knew in the pit of his heart that it was a disaster of some magnitude. All the men from the surrounding countryside supported each other through hard times, as did the women folk. Soon, they were joined by other men making their way to the lake, some carrying ropes and ladders, others, axes and picks – it meant only one thing. Someone had gone under the ice.

"Another hot flush dear?"

Confused, Rose awoke to find Alan placing a cup of tea on the bedside cabinet. "What – what time is it?"

"Just turned eight. Are you okay? You look very hot."

"Erm, yes, just a dream I think."

"Perhaps you're doing too much. Have a lazy morning. Oh, I might be late this evening, I'm collecting a spare part for my compressor on the way home. I'll ring when I'm half-an-hour away, that should give you time to prepare dinner. Bye Love."

With Alan now gone, she sat up and gathered her thoughts. Was it just a dream or was there more to it than that? Was it a premonition? Perhaps she should enquire at the next circle gathering; they had warned her that she might have strange moments when she felt things, but they hadn't explained what type of things they might be. Should she ring Shona, their leader? No, she didn't want to appear to be a nuisance; she'd ask when they met again on Wednesday. Her first task though, was to find her dream diary and write it all down before she forgot. Opening her notebook, she turned through the pages of her first entry, re-reading the plight of poor Joseph and Ester, then began a new chapter.

Feeling unsettled, Rose tried to go about her daily chores as usual, but her thoughts kept returning to last night's dream. What did it mean? Someone had gone under the ice. Was it John? How could she find out? A ringing phone broke into her reverie. By the time she reached it, the ringing had stopped and she had a missed call from Betty, a local woman who organised the pop-up-café in the village hall run by volunteers. Quicky, she returned the call.

"Hi Betty."

"Hello sweetie, I've put you down on the rota for waitressing duties next month. Also, would you bake those yummy chocolate buns again this week? The children loved them."

After hanging up Rose stared at her phone, should she contact her group? They did say to get in touch if she had any problems. Unsure of herself, she opened her WhatsApp group chat. There was a message from Shona.

Morning ladies, just to remind you all that we're meeting at Alison's house this week. Also, I thought it would be good if everyone could bring a small object along that has a special meaning to them.

Perfect. Smiling to herself Rose walked over to her newly acquired candlestick holders. She'd take one of them with her and tell the group about her dreams – they were sure to be able to offer her some much-needed advice.

4.

Wednesday morning dawned bright and sunny. Rose accepted the peck on her cheek and waved to Alan as he disappeared down the drive, a ritual that they had practised for almost thirty-seven years, but it wasn't quite the ritual that Rose had in mind this morning. No, this morning she wanted to practise mindfulness to prepare herself for the gathering. Turning to her new book of spells, she methodically followed the instructions, setting up her special altar to perform the new ritual. Carefully, she placed an earthenware bowl of rainwater on the small linen cloth, then lit her beeswax candles. Next came the fresh sprigs of lavender that she had picked from the garden – now she was ready. Sitting on the floor, she closed her eyes, took three deep breaths, and tried to empty her mind. But it was difficult. The first thought that burst through her concentration was about Alan. Had he remembered his packed lunch? Frustrated, she jumped up and opened the fridge door. No, he'd forgotten it again. That meant that he'd be ringing her when he realised, probably late morning, and he'd expect her to drop everything and take it into work for him. With dwindling enthusiasm, Rose returned to her altar to try again. Closing her eyes once more, she tried to visualise a stream gently tumbling over rounded boulders. This time she had more success, that was until she was interrupted by a text. Angry with herself for not turning her phone off, she succumbed to temptation. It could be from the group. But it wasn't.

Sorry Love, forgot my butties again. Any time before one will do. X

Beyond frustrated, Rose blew out the candles and decided a hot bath with lavender oil would probably be a better option, then she would set off a little earlier and drop the bloody sandwiches off on her way to Alison's house.

By the time she arrived she was feeling flustered. First, she'd been hampered by lumbering tractors, then the sat-nav had taken her to wrong address. But she was here now and determined to find answers to her questions. Nervously, she clutched the candlestick to her breast, walked up the garden path, rang the bell and waited, but no one came. Perhaps the bell didn't work. Yes, that must be it, so she knocked firmly on the wooden door, but again no one answered. Had she got the correct address? Fumbling in her bag she retrieved her phone to check the details then heard a cheery voice behind her.

"Hi Rose." Rose turned abruptly to be greeted by a familiar face – but the name wouldn't come. It wasn't Alison, she was much younger. "They'll be around the back in the summerhouse."

Trying to hide her nerves, Rose coughed and followed the familiar woman through a side gate into a rear garden. Stunned, Rose tried to take in the scene. It was a visual delight. The lawn had been turned into a buzzing wildflower meadow punctuated by trees laden with young fruits. Hens were roaming freely, pecking here and there at tasty morsels. Beyond the orchard lay a vegetable patch brimming with tempting fayre. A summer house set to the left, surrounded by flower beds led her wide eyes onto a magnificent pond with a surface like polished glass. Lost for words, Rose stared about her.

The woman at her side smiled. "Beautiful, isn't it?"

Alison's head popped out of the summer house. "Rose, Freya, welcome."

Overflowing with garden envy, Rose composed herself. "What an amazing garden you have."

"Thank you, and welcome. Do come in ladies. Shona's already here, the others will be along shortly."

Once inside, her eyes were again met with an equally stunning spectacle. The natural wooden interior was decorated with carvings of nymphs, sprites, and green men. On the window sills were vases laden with wildflowers. From the ceiling hung amulets and dried herbs while crystal balls of varying sizes and colours decorated the handmade table in the centre. Thinking back to this morning, Rose pictured her secret altar on the sideboard in their dining room. It looked pathetic at the side of this. Perhaps it wasn't good enough. Was that why she was unable to rid her mind of clutter this morning? But alas, she feared it had more to do with her newfound suspicions about her husband.

A glass of cold juice was pressed into the palm of her sweaty hand and she felt a light touch on her elbow as she was led to one of the giant floor cushions. "Rose, make yourself comfortable." It was Shona.

Alison was next, hovering over her with an elaborate vintage cake stand brimming with homemade treats. "Do have a cake, Rose. They're vegan."

Feeling way out of her depth, she somehow managed to compose herself and formulate a polite response. "Thank you. What a beautiful home you have."

Soon, Freya, who was now perched on a cushion at her side, took her hand. "Overwhelming, isn't it?" Nodding, Rose agreed, managing a weak smile. "Try to relax. We're a friendly group. Alison is fortunate to have all of this while I only live in a small, terraced house. It's not what you have, it's what you do that really counts."

Looking about her in awe, Rose watched silently as four more women arrived in a frenzy of floaty dresses, air kisses and hugs and made themselves comfortable. It was at this point that she noticed her candlestick was placed on the central table alongside several other objects. The banter quickly died down when Shona clashed two small brass cymbals together. It had begun.

Shona, as leader, began to chant a traditional rhyme. The women, all now sitting cross legged on their cushions with their eyes closed, joined in, repeating the words after her. Rose took a deep breath and followed suit. The cymbals crashed again, causing Rose to jump and open her eyes. Everyone was looking at her. Feeling her cheeks burn, she took a gulp of the cold juice clutched in her hands. It reminded her of her first day at infant school after being abandoned by her mother. The sultry, humid atmosphere wasn't helping matters either.

"Welcome each and every one of you."

The group of women, sitting tall and straight, all bowed their heads towards Shona. Shuffling uncomfortably, trying not to fall off her giant cushion, Rose did the same.

"Ladies first let's get rid of all the negativity in the room. I want you to picture a deep, inky black pool, then I want you to think of all the everyday burdens that you're carrying with you and cast them into its depths. Ready? Do it now." Rose immediately pictured Alan. Feeling guilty and uncomfortable, knowing full well that she couldn't throw him into the pond, she tried to picture something else. But nothing would come. "There, that's better," Shona continued, but Rose wasn't keeping up.

"Now, you might be wondering why I asked you all to

bring a special object." All of the eyes on Shona were devouring her every word but Rose was still thinking about tossing Alan and his bloody buttie box into the water. But now it wasn't just a garden pond, it was a raging river in full spate. "Alison, as you're today's host, perhaps you would go first."

Rose was aware of Alison's voice in the background, but was clueless as to its content, Alan was now clinging to the side of a lifeboat being tossed about in the deep, black ocean and she could see menacing icebergs floating past his head.

"Thank you, Alison, that was very interesting, but ladies, I'm afraid I'm going to have to stop you there." Several perfectly plucked eyebrows raised in unison while Shona scanned the women sat around her. "Someone is having difficulties." The raised eyebrows quickly morphed into looks of concern as the group began to glance at each other questioningly. Rose's blush deepened to resemble the poppies in the vase next to her. How could she get out of this one? She couldn't possibly tell this group of strangers that she suspected that her husband was having an affair and her marriage was about to hit the rocks. Sighing, she took a sip of her juice, trying to buy herself some more time, then it came to her. Hot flush. Yes, she was having a hot flush caused by the menopause.

"I'm so sorry, my menopause symptoms are causing me trouble at the moment."

Freya jumped up and was at her side in no time offering her more cold juice, then Alison stood up and disappeared into the garden out of sight. Embarrassed, Rose struggled to her feet, "Perhaps I should go?"

"Not at all my dear. Let's relocate under the weeping willow, it's always cooler under there." Shona put her arm under Rose's elbow and steered her to the bottom of the impressive garden where they reached the generous shade of the old tree. "There, that's better."

Not enjoying the attention, Rose began to feel foolish. What was she doing here? What on earth possessed her to think she was a witch? This was so far outside of her comfort zone.

"Don't doubt yourself." It was Freya's reassuring voice whispering quietly in her ear again.

'How on earth does Freya know I'm doubting myself?' Rose wondered, but didn't voice her thoughts.

Alison was now back with a small, brown glass bottle containing a homemade potion. "Rub this onto the inside of your wrists and elbows three times a day, it will help with the symptoms." Once more Rose found herself doubting the potion. If the HRT medication from her GP wasn't helping then this surely wouldn't either.

"It works wonders, I promise. My mum swears by it. It got her through the menopause."

How did these women know what was going through her mind? Perhaps they really were witches after all.

Inspired by Alison's garden, she called at the florists on her way home and chose a bunch of colourful summer flowers to place in her new German vase. After arranging them carefully, she placed the vase on the sideboard alongside her altar, breathing in the heady scent, relieved to be back safely in her cosy cottage.

Later that night when insomnia struck, Rose laid in bed listening to Alans's snoring, getting more and more frustrated with herself. Then the naggings doubts returned. Was he seeing another woman? Possibly someone from his motorsport club. A few women did compete, Rose had met a couple of them, sisters apparently. One drove and the other navigated. He had a perfect alibi. But he wouldn't cheat on her, would he? Eventually, she gave up and went for a fresh glass of iced water, taking it into the spare bedroom, where her thoughts returned once more to the meeting. Images of Alison's flowing black hair and almond shaped, hazel eyes along with her immaculate home and garden infiltrated her brain causing her to doubt herself once more. Was she good enough to become a witch? Was it something you could just decide to be, or were you born different? How would she know? Finally, with her head in spin, she fell into a deep sleep.

5.

Phil beamed. "Target in view, are you ready Hank?"

"Sure thing."

The two men drove slowly down the lane in an orange Ford Cortina and approached a young woman wearing a red leather miniskirt paired with black knee length boots, "Well hello Ma'am, do you want a ride? We're heading into town."

The woman stopped and smiled. "Why not." Once she'd climbed in the back and adjusted her skirt she leaned forward. "Not seen you around here before. Are you from the base?"

"Yes Ma'am, I'm David and the ugly one is Mick. And you are?"

"Sabine."

"Sabine – that's a real pretty name."

Sabine leaned back and shrank down in her seat, her mind now in turmoil. The enemy. She couldn't be seen fraternising with the enemy.

"Want a smoke?" One of the men leaned over, passing her a joint.

Sabine's face lit up. One night wouldn't matter. Nobody

would know. It got rather lonely at the camp with no men around and it was a long trek into town.

"Thanks." Sabine held the cigarette up to her nose and nodded happily before taking it between her lips and inhaling deeply. Wacky baccy. It had been a while.

"There's plenty more where that came from." The guy took a swig from an open bottle of Jack Daniels then offered it to Sabine. "Want to find somewhere to pull over and party?"

The Ford Cortina carried on further up the lane and pulled off next to a wooded area. Sabine got out, teetering on her high heels. "This grass is really strong."

"Sure is the best." The shorter of the two men winked at his accomplice, took Sabine by the arm and led her into the trees.

The trio reached a small clearing where they sat down, and before long, Sabine was laid on her back giggling, gazing at the stars. But it wasn't long before their silvery sparkle turned into whirling psychedelic patterns.

Hungry for air Rose coughed and pushed the covers off, looking about her into the gloom. The spare room, yes, she was safe in the spare room. But somebody wasn't safe! Her heartrate spiked as she tried to recall her brief dream. Drugged. She'd been drugged. But who was Sabine and how could she help her? Sick to her stomach she paced the room, furious with herself for not being able to help. What should she do, go to the police? Flopping back down on the bed she sighed realising how ridiculous that would sound. This incident probably took place way back in the past, long before the notion of having your drink spiked was a thing. Amy and Vicky, her two, precious daughters sprang into her mind. She needed to contact them, she needed to know they were safe. What time was it? Five-fifteen – it was way too early, anyway, it was Thursday morning; neither of her girls went out during the week. No, they would both be tucked up, snuggled safely in their beds.

Opening the blinds, trying to calm her mind, Rose stared out onto the front lawn. The grass was neatly mown to within an inch of its life. Barren. But that's how Alan liked it. Thinking of Alan did nothing to lift her spirits, so she pulled on her robe and went to the kitchen in search of chamomile tea. That usually helped.

By the time Alan appeared for breakfast, Rose was still feeling frustrated. She needed to talk to someone. But who? She couldn't confide in Alan; he'd probably laugh and tell her to stop being ridiculous. No, it had to be someone that understood. That left her with no choice but someone from the circle. All the girls seemed friendly enough, but there did appear to be a bit of a clique. Everyone coveted Shona's attention, but it was clear that Shona and Alison were friends. Rose closed her eyes, and an image of Freya came into her head. Yes, Freya. She seemed more like the sort of person she could relate to. For a start she was older, but not as old as Rose. Probably in her mid-forties if she had to guess. And she wasn't tall and willowy with a figure to die for. No, she was a middle-aged woman with a fuller figure more akin to her own. "Yes," she whispered to herself, "I'll text Freya when I've finished baking."

The morning wore on and Rose was busy decorating the chocolate muffins for the pop-up-café when her phone rang. Annoyed, she wiped her hands down her apron expecting to see Alan's number, but she was wrong. What a coincidence, it was Freya.

"Good morning, Rose. I hope you don't mind me ringing you. Is it a convenient time to chat?"

"No, erm, yes, erm, I mean, it's okay Freya, thank you for ringing. I'm just decorating chocolate muffins."

"Yummy, my favourite."

Rose knew this was the perfect opportunity to ask for her help. Taking a deep breath, she plucked up the courage and continued. "Freya, please come over and sample a few. In fact, I er…, I was hoping to ask your advice. When are you free?"

"Give me an hour."

Hurriedly, Rose tidied the kitchen then ran a comb through her greying hair. This really was bizarre; she'd been thinking about Freya earlier and then she rang! Was it just a coincidence?

Awkwardly stepping forward, Rose wondered how she should greet Freya, but the decision was taken from her when the friendly woman leaned in for a hug. "Rose, thank you for inviting me, what an amazing cottage."

Once in the kitchen, Freya casually dropped her bag on the floor and sat in the old rocking chair. "I bet this chair has some fascinating stories to tell. How old is it?"

Cocking her head to one side, Rose considered the question. "I have no idea; it was already here when we came. I sent a message to the previous occupant, but he said it belonged here."

Closing her eyes, Freya took a deep breath and leaned back into its polished wooden spindles. "And so it does."

"Alan thinks it should go to the tip; he doesn't want it in the kitchen."

Alarmed, Freya's head snapped up. "No! You can't do that. It's an amazing piece of furniture."

"It's very tatty and splashed with paint. A few of the spindles are damaged too."

Leaning forward Freya raised her eyebrows. "It's special Rose. Don't ever get rid of it."

Trying to disguise her bemusement, Rose gestured towards the lounge. "Would you like to come through?"

"I like it well enough here, thank you."

Feeling even more confused, Rose poured the coffee and offered Freya a muffin.

"You chose one for me."

Rose decided that she now knew what Alice had felt like when she'd ventured down the rabbit hole, faltering before handing her one with the least sprinkles, now wondering if they were a little too childish. "I've, er, made them for the charity café tomorrow. The children usually pop in on their way home from school."

"They look delicious Rose." When Rose set the tray down Freya took hold of her hand and she found herself peering into a pair of sparkling, emerald-green eyes with a feline quality to them. "Don't doubt yourself, you're as good as the rest of the members - have a little more self-belief, Rose. And don't be put off by their beauty. You and I both know it won't last the journey."

Lost for words Rose tried to formulate a sensible response. She failed. "But, er, I, er..."

"Just take strength from your gut instinct Rose, to know who is worthy of your time - and celebrate your uniqueness - the very thing that makes you who you are."

Sitting back, Freya took a bite from the muffin making appreciative noises, giving Rose time to digest her words.

After composing herself, Rose was the first one to break the long silence. "Thank you for coming Freya, I'm feeling a little confused and wondered if you could help me."

"I will if I can."

"It's just that, well, I, erm…" faltering again, Rose sighed and glanced out of the window into the back garden. How could she possibly tell this woman that she barely knew about the weird visions that she'd been having recently? Like the one she'd had last night about poor Sabine. How could she explain?

Once more, Freya leaned forward and took her companion's hand. "Let me guess – you're still questioning if you're good enough to be a real witch?"

"Well - partly."

"Okay," Freya sat back and smiled, then continued, "what exactly is a witch?" Surprised by the question Rose looked back wide eyed. "I'll tell you – it's just a word. A noun to be exact, like dog or chair; a word that gives an object an identity."

Wondering where this was going, Rose listened intently as her friend picked up another cake. "Take this cake for instance – how do you know it's good enough to be called a cupcake?" Rose felt even more confused than ever now as she watched Freya devour the object, "Because it's delicious. Don't you see? You are amazing! Witch is just the word used to describe a person who lives by a certain set of beliefs. We can't perform magic – nobody can. We can only do things to the best of our ability. We try to be the best that we can – live sustainably, lend a hand, do the right thing, but we're normal people Rose."

"But what about the spells and rituals?"

Freya's face relaxed and her emerald eyes shone once more, "Think of them as prayers Rose. If you believed in God you would pray in a church, if you have witchy beliefs, you perform spells, meditations and rituals, but it's not magic - it's energy."

Suddenly, Rose felt a little lighter, then a frown creased her brow when she thought about her altar. Jumping up, she took Freya's hand and led her into the dining room. "This is my altar, but I don't think I've got it right. And my crystal ball - I think it might be too small."

"You don't need a crystal ball Rose; I haven't got one." Freya watched as she observed her friend struggling with the information. "Crystals are just stones wearing a frilly dress. I collect mine from the land around us. Go and take a walk by the river, you'll be surprised what you find. There are so many polished pebbles and rocks. Take what you need and return them when you've finished. But remember to thank the river and leave a small offering - like seeds or nuts for the birds that live there."

Rose's mouth dropped open as she tried to take in Freya's words of wisdom. "But there were several beautiful crystal balls at Alison's…"

"Ornaments, nothing more, Rose, commercial trappings to part you from your money. You can empty your mind and gaze into a roaring fire or stare at the clouds. Even a puddle would suffice. You don't need to buy crystal balls and trinkets. Think about the stone circles that you've seen – are they made from polished crystals Rose? No, they aren't." Freya paused for a moment to let Rose's thoughts catch up, "You don't even need an altar – just a quiet space where you feel safe and comfortable. I have a special house plant on my window sill that I sit next to when I feel the need, it seems to give me positive energy. In return I feed and water it. It's a symbiotic relationship. We take care of the earth, and the earth takes care of us."

Rose felt her shoulders drop as she looked about the dining room. Freya had given her plenty to think about. Cheerily, she changed the subject. "This is my favourite room."

"The light in here is amazing. Why don't you put that old rocking chair near the patio doors? It would be perfect?"

Frowning, Rose thought about the chair; it was hard and

uncomfortable. "I'm not so sure, it's a bit - knobbly."

"The next time you go into town, get some fabric and make a few cushions for it. You don't need to spend much. See what you can find in the charity shop. Now, let me help you to lift it through."

With the chair in its new position Freya hugged Rose, "I'll see you next Wednesday at the meeting, and don't fret – all will eventually become clear."

With mixed feelings Rose watched her friend walk down the drive, climb onto a rickety old bicycle and cycle away into the sunshine. Freya had certainly given her plenty to think about, but she hadn't asked her about the dreams. What did they mean? And just what would eventually become clear?

6.

The weekend was looming and for once Alan wasn't attending an event. What should they do? There were plenty of jobs that needed to be addressed, but most of them required professionals like plumbers and electricians; they couldn't tackle those jobs, but they could do something with the garden. The front was formal, neat and tidy with a few small borders and a generous sized lawn, but it had potential. The back however was more utilitarian, a place for their dog to play between the cavernous double garage and oversized workshop, which left little room for planting – the very reason why Alan wanted the property in the first place. He hadn't fallen for the charming, old building and its history, like Rose had. Sighing, she walked outside into the sunshine and wandered full circle around the cottage, trying to picture how she could emulate Alison's wonderful outside space. She'd discuss it with him this evening. Perhaps they could even eat at the pub in the village for a change.

"It's not our wedding anniversary, is it?" Alan asked cautiously, taking his first sip of chilled Chardonnay.

Shaking her head, Rose picked up the menu. "No, that was last month Alan. I just thought it was a nice way to start the weekend together." Glancing over the top of the menu, she smiled nervously. It was now or never. "I was thinking we could take a look at the front garden…" But she didn't get chance to finish.

"There's nothing wrong with the front garden. I like it as it is."

"No, but there's nothing right with it either. It's dull." A thought sprang into her mind and she wanted to carry on and say, 'Just like you' but she didn't. "I'd like a small wildlife pond and some fruit trees, and we could turn some of the lawn into a wildflower meadow."

"I'm not so sure Rose; it would look, well, messy."

A young waitress arrived to take their order, buying her time to gain some fortitude and trust her gut instincts while taking a few gulps of cold wine for added courage. "Can't you see? It's alright for you Alan, you've got your man cave, well two of them actually, full of expensive toys. What have I got?"

Shocked, Alan sat and looked at his wife, really looked at her for the first time in a long while. Was she unhappy? Hadn't he given her everything she needed, lovely home, two beautiful daughters? She'd even got a dog now that the girls had both left. She didn't need to work. What more could she possibly want? Not quite knowing what to say, he shuffled awkwardly in his chair.

With the wine now coursing through her veins Rose continued, "I don't mean to sound ungrateful, but I'd like the front garden to be my domain, to do as I wish. You've got the back."

Realising he was now on thin ice, Alan conceded and took her hand. "Okay, let's draw up some plans tomorrow and decide what to do."

Sleep was hard to find; Rose listened to Edward signalling every hour. She couldn't decide if it was the adrenaline rush of standing up for herself, or the fact that she was going to get her wildlife garden that was keeping her awake. Whichever it was, she was feeling empowered.

True to his word, after breakfast, they were out in the front garden with a long tape measure and Alan's iPad and, by lunchtime, they had a rough plan. There was room for five or six small fruit trees on the lawn, and a medium sized pond would fit well at the bottom of the front garden where it gently sloped away into a shrubby area. Perfect. All they needed now was someone to dig the big hole for the pond. The trees and meadow area she could tackle herself.

A week later she'd had two quotes for the pond, but they were both eye-wateringly expensive. Why would it cost so much to dig a hole and line it with rubber? Time for plan B. The next evening, Rose walked down the village to introduce herself to Jim, the local builder. Betty from the café had told her that he had a mini digger and would probably dig her a hole for beer money – whatever that was! She was in luck. He'd come at the weekend; all she had to do was hire a skip for the spoil, mark out the area to be excavated and line his back pocket with cash. Deal done, she felt exhilarated - she'd sorted it out for herself without Alans's help.

The day dawned bright and breezy and Alan was away again, but for once she didn't mind; his fancy woman – if he had one – was welcome to him! And he hadn't even mentioned the pond when he'd left earlier. Rose was once more beginning to doubt herself. Had she bitten off more than she could chew? Could she project manage her little venture without his help? The thought of Alan leaving her caused her to break out in a sweat. How would she manage without him? What would they tell the girls?

"Pull yourself together woman!" she chastised herself. "You've got an hour until Jim arrives." So, she strolled around the front garden, taking deep breaths, trying to envisage it full of birdsong and the buzz of insects foraging in her mini meadow. Yes, she decided, she could do this.

Eight-thirty came and went with no sign of Jim and his digger; she was beginning to worry. Would he let her down? How could she attend the next meeting on Wednesday? They would think her stupid and incapable after telling them all about her plans. Feeling deflated, she stepped over the string line on the lawn marking out the area to be excavated, sat cross legged and closed her eyes, trying to imagine the pond beneath her. It took her a while to clear her mind, but eventually she relaxed, took a deep breath and forgot about Jim and his digger.

Her nostrils immediately filled with a pungent aroma; it wasn't unpleasant, but she couldn't place it. Trying hard, she inhaled deeper and began to feel warm, tingling sensations traveling up through the damp earth into her body, first into her buttocks, but then it spread quickly into her torso. The aroma, now deep in her lungs reminded her of something, but what? A smell from long ago, somewhere lodged in the distant past. Hay and raisins. An earthy scent, sweet and mellow. A faded image teased the inside of her eyelids. A musty room, backlit by the sun, with a man gazing out of the window. Who was he?

"Morning, sorry we're a bit late." Shocked back to the present, Rose opened her eyes; it was Jim. He had a young lad with him. "This is Charlie, my apprentice."

Momentarily confused, Rose stood up quickly, causing a dizzy spell.

"Are you okay miss?" It was Charlie, stepping forward, taking her hand to steady her.

"Yes, yes, I'm fine. Sorry, I didn't hear you arrive."

Jim just nodded, secretly wondering if she was deaf. How on earth hadn't she heard his digger rattling around in the back of his pickup.

The turf was off in no time and the pond was beginning to take shape. Excitedly, Rose was issuing instructions where she wanted the pond to have a sloping side to make a pebble beach and underwater shelves for aquatic plants to grow. Rose's other task it seemed was to provide endless drinks and to try and get Jim to follow her instructions – apparently, he'd never previously dug out a pond and was under the impression that all that was required was a hole. His enthusiasm however made up for his lack of knowledge. By lunchtime the hole was nearly a meter deep in the middle and they'd hit something buried in a layer of yellow clay.

Concerned, Rose moved closer to inspect it. "Oh dear! Is that our water supply?"

Taking off his flat cap and scratching his head, Jim climbed down out of his machine. "No love, don't worry, it's old land drainage. There's lots of it 'round 'ere. Use to be farmland y' see. We've 'it the clay now."

"Will it be okay?"

"Course, Love. I come across 'em all't time in this area. They don't run anymore, clogged up, see."

Jim lifted out a short section of the old terracotta pipe and handed it to Rose, it was indeed clogged up with sticky clay. Charlie took it from her and carried it to the skip where all the rest of the discarded material lay.

"'Appen we've finished now, Love," Jim added with a nod, before retrieving his tools and loading his digger back onto his truck.

Happy with the amount of beer money offered, Jim and Charlie left with a cheery wave while Rose surveyed the area. It looked like a scene from a war film in the trenches. Mud and clay everywhere. The lawn was churned up where the digger had sat, and a trail of sticky clay clung to the surface of the drive all the way down to the skip. But she had her hole. It would need some tweaking of course. The beach area was way too steep, the pebbles would just slide off into the depths and the planting shelf was uneven, but it was a starting place. She could work with it. Her priority now though would have to be the mess on the drive. Alan would be back tomorrow afternoon and he'd blow a fuse if his beloved Alfa-Romeo had to paddle through the mud.

After a hasty lunch, she was back out in the garden with a brush and shovel, attempting to clean the long drive, but the clay was tenacious, stuck like tar to the block paving and squashed in tightly between the gaps. An hour later and it didn't look much better. What could she do? She didn't hear her phone ringing where she'd left it on the doorstep. She was too engrossed setting up the hosepipe to try and blast the pesky stuff away. It didn't improve matters, though. The water separated the mud from the clay, causing it to run in gloopy rivulets over the surface, making it look more like a landslide. Exasperated, she sat down on the wall with her head in her hands; she'd got twenty-four hours to redress the issue before Alan returned. Time to call in a professional. Reaching for her phone she noticed a missed call from Alan. What did he want? He didn't usually ring during the day when competing at his events.

"Sorry, I missed your call, is everything okay?"

The colour drained from Rose's face. He'd suffered a broken prop shaft and had retired early from the event and would be back in an hour. Disaster. There was nothing she could do except brace herself for his wrath.

Alan didn't disappoint, he made her feel like a naughty schoolgirl. "What were you thinking Rose? How on earth could you let this happen?" These were just a couple of his many beratings. By suppertime, though, the drive was sanitised and the lawn had been rolled like a sheet of filo pastry, exactly as he liked it. Order. She, on the other hand, seemed to live with constant chaos. Tomorrow they would address the hole, which Alan pointed out wasn't level and needed to be banked up at one side or the water would just pour out.

7.

Alan retreated into the garage for what was left of the evening and Rose decided it was the best place for him. Sighing, she pulled on a fleece and went out into her front garden. The sun was setting, and the sky was a blazing orange, illuminating the side of the cavernous yellow skip, making it appear almost attractive in a weird sort of way. Drawn to it, she leaned over and plunged her hands into the mountain of earth. Realising it was too valuable a resource to waste – she would, after all, need some topsoil to landscape her wildlife garden - she gathered several sturdy sacks and began to fill them, dropping stones and unwanted pieces of rubble into a bucket. Satisfied with her efforts, Rose picked up the half full bucket and was just about to tip it back into the skip when something caught her eye. Was it a shell? Retrieving the object, she took it to the outside tap to rinse away the mud, slowly revealing her find. It was the bowl of an old clay pipe. Traces of mud engrained into its surface highlighted a rough pattern carved on it. Fascinated, Rose took the item inside and gently washed it with an old toothbrush. There was some writing, possibly someone's initials, but what did it say? It was discoloured and worn. Squinting, she held it up to the light. It definitely began with a K, or was it a H? There was another letter, it could be another K or was it M? Frustrated and excited, she placed it on the window sill to dry, put the kettle on and called Alan in.

It was time for bed.

Another sleepless night. This time, Rose was haunted by the image of the old man that she'd seen earlier. Who was he? And what did he have to do with her? So many questions - first Ester and Joseph, then Alice and Jack, followed by Sabine and now this. Who were these people and what did they have to do with her? And Freya. What did she mean by, *'All will eventually become clear?'*

Edward's chimes alerted Rose to the fact that it was three in the morning and she was still wide awake. She couldn't blame Alan's snoring; he was, for once, as quiet as a mouse. No, something strange was happening to her, and she needed to get to the bottom of it. But how? She knew that Freya was somehow involved but it seemed like she wasn't going to tell her. It was something she had to work out for herself. Frustrated, she made a mug of hot chocolate. Turning, her eyes landed on the small clay pipe still on the window sill in the utility room where she'd left it. Who had it belonged to? Jim said it used to be farmland so presumably it had been lost by a farmer. But when? And how old was it? Sipping her drink, she opened her laptop and began her research.

It appeared that clay pipes could be identified and dated by their pattern and size; the smaller the bowl the older the pipe. Some pipes had the maker's initial below the bowl. Enthusiastically, Rose turned the pipe over to examine it closely. The bowl seemed small to her and there definitely was someone's initials, but they were worn and difficult to read. An hour later, and with growing frustration, she was no wiser. Time to go back to bed.

When Rose woke, there was no sign of Alan. What time was it? Turned nine! She never slept this late. After dressing hurriedly, she found him in the front garden with his laser level, surveying the hole.

"The far side needs raising by thirty-two centimetres, we need to build a bank. There's plenty of spoil in the skip."

Rose sighed and nodded, remembering that he'd always been a perfectionist. Was his mistress perfect as well, she wondered? She knew he wouldn't want a divorce, but could she learn to live with his extracurricular activities?

"Rose!" His sharp voice brought her back. "Pass me the shovel."

By evening the underlay and thick rubber liner were in place and they were ready to turn on the hose. After supper the pond was full and all that remained was to trim and tidy the edges.

"Better leave that until one evening later in the week to give the earth time to settle."

THE WITCH'S CHAIR

Excited, Rose spent the next couple of days at the garden, centre choosing native plants for her new pond and researching fruit trees and wildlife meadows. The time flew by, and Wednesday morning arrived again. It was Freya's turn to host. She'd texted her address, so all Rose had to do was to find somewhere to park, but Freya's house was on the busy main road into town; there was no drive and not even a front garden. Rose was both excited and a little anxious as she knocked on the door of the tiny, terraced house. Freya stepped out from the green painted door and hugged her.

"Lovely to see you again, thank you for coming."

Stepping inside, Rose tried not to look around or stare. The small room was sparsely furnished, with an old-fashioned leather sofa and one armchair and an even older side table. In one alcove sat an outdated television and the other alcove housed shelves stuffed with musty books. Beneath her feet, the wooden floor was draped with a red rug in front of an open fireplace.

"I thought we'd sit outside. Got to make the most of what's left of summer; the days are shortening."

Rose followed Freya through the compact kitchen and out into a cosy courtyard.

"Oh, it's lovely Freya. Have you created this yourself?" Rose asked, gesturing to the pots and tubs overflowing with ferns and hostas.

"Yes, but it's very shady so unfortunately I can't grow many flowers."

Freya stepped back into the kitchen to collect the cafetiere and croissants while Rose continued surveying the small space. It was enchanting. Ivy clung to the high brick walls concealing nesting boxes and bird feeders. An old mossy stone bowl full of water rested on top of an ancient tree stump. It felt calm and serene. Freya set two cups and plates on the small iron table and poured the coffee while Rose's eyes continued glancing around her new surroundings.

"I, er, didn't know if we were supposed to bring anything with us so I've brought this old clay pipe that I found in the garden."

Taking it from her, Freya held it to her nose and inhaled deeply then cupped it in her hands and closed her eyes. Rose observed as several expressions rippled across her face before she opened her eyes again.

"That's very interesting Rose, thank you."

"Sadly, I don't know how old it is or who it belonged to. I couldn't find much on the internet."

"Well, it's certainly old. Can I take a photo of it?"

Nodding, Rose smiled, "Please do."

Looking at the image on her phone, Freya concentrated as she uploaded it onto an archaeology website. "Someone will be able to tell us about it."

'Why didn't I think of that?' Rose mused to herself, then a bigger question popped into her head. Where were the others? She'd been here at least half-an-hour. Where were Alison and Shona and the rest of the group?

Freya's emerald eyes met Rose's. "No one else is coming Rose."

"What...what do you mean? Why aren't they coming?"

Shrugging, Freya picked up her cup and averted her eyes. "Only Shona turns up when it's my turn to host, but she's got an appointment this morning."

Surprised and shocked, Rose was about to question Freya further, but she cut her off. "Ooh, look, we've got a response already." Scrolling through her phone Freya continued, "Apparently your pipe is possibly from Kilkenny in Ireland, you can tell by the pattern and initials. And, as I thought, it's old."

With thoughts of the others now forgotten, Rose leaned in to see more. "Wow! It's from the eighteen-fifties. Do you think it's worth anything?"

Shuffling forward, Freya touched her hand. "It will have little, if any, monetary value, but it almost certainly belonged to someone's ancestor."

Rose instantly felt ridiculous for asking. What did it matter if it had value? She wouldn't ever consider selling it; it belonged to her cottage, and that's where it would stay.

"I wonder what else is buried in the garden?"

Considering her question, Freya leaned back and sighed. "Lots of things I expect, the everyday objects of the people that have gone before. We don't truly own anything Rose; we're just custodians of our possessions. We can't take anything with us when we die."

This made Rose think about the objects she'd bought at the antiques fair, Edward, the candlesticks and the German vase. Yes, they'd all previously belonged to others. Those people would now be long dead. Freya was right, we never truly owned anything.

"Mm, when I die, what will Amy and Vicky do with my possessions? What a sobering thought."

"I'm sure they'll treasure some of them Rose."

A strange though popped into Rose's head; she knew nothing about Freya, she had always managed to keep the conversation firmly about Rose. This needed to be rectified.

"So, Freya, tell me about your family. Do you have any children?"

Fidgeting a little on her chair, Freya turned to watch as a robin landed in the bowl of water to bathe. "Nature is my family Rose, the birds and the insects."

An awkward silence followed and Rose pondered why Freya wouldn't tell her anything. And why had none of the others turned up?

Standing, Freya put her hand on Rose's shoulder, signalling the end of the meeting. "Well, thank you for coming and showing me your clay pipe Rose. I'll see you next week."

8.

Frustrated and confused Rose tried to concentrate on her garden as summer gradually turned into autumn. The meetings continued, but as yet she hadn't hosted any of them. Apparently, the rule was that you had to have been a member for a year before you were considered committed or experienced enough. There were times when she felt as though she was a real witch, like the day that she planted her fruit trees, saying a traditional blessing as each one was lowered ceremoniously into the prepared earth. She could feel and see the magic happening before her very eyes when her mini wildflower meadow burst into flower, attracting a myriad of insects into its beating heart. Colourful dragon and damsel flies flitted across the surface of her new pond; all of these things brought her great joy. But she was still haunted at night by her recurrent dreams. What did they mean? She was no further forward, and Freya wasn't much help. Whenever she questioned her, she had a knack of changing the subject.

"Have you made those cushions yet for your rocking chair?" She'd lost count of how many times she'd asked her that question. Alan wasn't overly happy to find the chair in the dining room and had banished it into the garden. When the first of the autumnal storms rolled in from the Atlantic, aptly named storm Alan, it took with it the leaves from her young fruit trees, and, as Rose collected them to make leaf mould, she knew it was time to leave the garden to sleep and return to her indoor tasks.

The next meeting was at Shona's, and everyone was present and eager.

"Welcome sisters, let us waste no time; we've got a lot to get through this morning."

Immediately, everyone assumed their position on the cushions, closed their eyes and bowed their heads as Shona opened the meeting with a chant. Rose, tried to clear her mind but it seemed, as always, that the harder she tried, the more difficult it became. The first wayward thought that grabbed her attention was her shopping list that she'd been writing this morning; she needed more chocolate sprinkles for her cakes for the pop-up-cafe. Screwing her eyes tight shut, she managed to dislodge that thought, only for it to be replaced by another. Alan. It was his birthday in a couple of weeks, and she still hadn't got him a present. He'd always been difficult to buy for; the only thing he ever wanted was tools or car parts, and what fun was there in buying those? He usually ordered them online anyway and never wanted her to wrap them for him. Thoughts of Alan then turned into suspicion. Was he seeing someone else? What would his mistress buy him for his birthday and where would he hide it? What should she do? She couldn't possibly mention it to Amy or Vicky.

Amy, like her father, was pragmatic and would probably take it in her stride, but Vicky had always been a sensitive soul, like her mother.

"I'm sure that you don't need me to remind you ladies, that we're fast approaching the full moon."

Shona's words brought her back to the room, where all eyes were fixed on their leader, as though she held a great power. Perhaps she did. But why then, Rose mused, couldn't she feel it? The only meeting where she'd ever felt anything remotely powerful was when she was sitting in Freya's small courtyard garden. Shona continued her sermon and then the group were invited to join her in a ritual blessing to the moon as she transformed from Maiden to Mother, the giver of new life. This week's homework was, of course, to celebrate the coming of the full moon.

"I'll email everyone my vegan recipe for moon cookies."

The word vegan reverberated in Rose's head. She didn't eat meat but had oily fish twice a week. Did she need to give that up too? And what about eggs? Her next thought was of her trying to persuade Alan not to eat anymore meat. He had ham sandwiches on a regular basis and loved pork pies and sausages. She should know, she'd packed up his butty box for nearly four decades. She even used to do it when she worked.

"Don't overthink it Rose," Freya's words interrupted her thoughts, "ring if you want to talk."

THE WITCH'S CHAIR

Rose wasn't sure what she was supposed to do to celebrate the full moon. She'd always been aware of it throughout her life and had noticed that she usually had difficulty sleeping when there was a full moon, though she'd never previously spent much time pondering the situation. What should she do? She had a few days to prepare, it was this coming Saturday, and thankfully Alan would be away.

The mornings were getting darker as the wheel of life continued turning, and, after waving Alan off, Rose heaved a sigh of relief. She had the rest of the day to prepare for her first full moon ritual. For once she was grateful that he was absent. She couldn't possibly practise any form of spirituality in his presence. He would think she'd gone mad.

Her first task was to cleanse her body. The cool morning air kissed her skin as she went about cutting her favourite herbs; they were beginning to look tired now and would wither and curl at the first frosts. Then she ran a hot bath and immersed the herbs into the water while visualising the energy being released from them. Next, she returned to the bedroom for her bathrobe. Feeling a little irritated she stopped, noticing that Alan had discarded his jacket on the floor, most unlike him. Holding it up to her face she inhaled deeply, could she smell perfume or was it in her imagination? Taking another sniff, she began to panic. Yes! Yes she could, and it wasn't hers, she never used perfume. A thought popped into her head. Should she look through his pockets? The feeling was quickly replaced with guilt. He'd never given her cause to doubt him previously. They'd been married for thirty-seven years and had been happy. So why did she feel differently now? No, she wasn't going to spoil her day with negative thoughts.

Feeling invigorated after her bath, she continued her preparations, making a nourishing, homemade broth from the seasonal vegetables she'd bought at the local farmers market to go with the organic loaf that she'd made. Simple country fayre. In the afternoon she took her dog, Nellie, for a long walk in the countryside, trying to keep her thoughts on the wonderful things surrounding her. The fields, now harvested, were peppered with hungry geese, exhausted after their long migration. The trees, almost bare looked stark against the cloudy sky. "Cloudy sky!" The words stuck in her throat as she shouted them. How could she perform a full moon celebration if she couldn't see the moon? Panicking, she text Freya. But her reply was reassuring.

Don't get hung up on it Rose, the moon is powerful, even if you can't see her, you know she's still there.

Back home she had an early supper, more homemade broth. The hedge witch recipe that she'd used said that it nourished and cleansed the body and soul, perfect for this evening's ceremony. Excited, she pulled on a fleece and took her chosen objects outside into the front garden. Her garden. Her handbook suggested that she should have white sage, but the only sage she had was common garden sage that she'd dried and tied into a bundle. It also called for the semi-precious stone, labradorite. Rose didn't have any of that either so took her crystal ball outside with her; it was made from selenite, which was another of the stones suggested. She had also slipped into her pocket a small heart shaped stone which she treasured; her daughter, Vicky, had given it to her many years earlier.

First, she perched warily on the edge of the new bench next to her pond and glanced about her. It was almost dark and lights were beginning to go on in the other houses in the village. What would the neighbours think if they saw her? Would they all talk about her? Sitting back, she tried to relax and clear her mind, but as usual she found it a difficult task. Sighing, she opened her eyes, to be met by a cheery smile.

"Hello Rose, a bit chilly, isn't it?" It was Betty, out walking her dog.

Startled, she waved back. "Yes, I hope it isn't going to rain."

With Betty now gone, she tried again, only to be thwarted a few minutes later by the noise of a car driving past. And she couldn't see the moon. Frustrated, and feeling rather self-conscious, she gathered her things together, went into the back garden and placed them on the table outside the patio doors leading into the dining room. It wasn't the setting she'd envisaged, but at least it was private. Shivering, she popped inside for her coat and helped herself to a generous glass of Malbec.

"Oh, well, I might as well have another go. What do you think Nellie?" Nellie, her little dog didn't reply but went and sat next to the rocking chair with pleading eyes. "Really? You want me to sit on that?"

Cocking her head to one side, Nellie let out a whiny sound.

"Okay, let me grab a blanket to sit on; it's not very comfortable."

Once seated, Rose tried again. The first thing she noticed was a cold feeling in her buttocks, probably the damp wood, she thought. After all, the chair had been outside for a few weeks now. Perhaps she should put it in the garden shed to keep it dry over the coming winter. Closing her eyes, she made a fist around the small heart shaped stone in her left hand, chanting, "Left to leave and right to receive." Mm, now she was even more confused. Should she be giving to, or receiving from the moon? About to go back inside for her phone, she stopped herself. She couldn't possibly text Freya now. No, she'd probably be in a trance like state, or would she be singing while performing a special dance? Trying to picture her friend, Rose screwed her eyes tight shut and concentrated. Freya would be doing whatever felt right for her, and that's exactly what Rose began to do. Quietly at first, almost in a whisper, she began saying all of the words as they came into her head one by one. "Alan, Amy, Vicky. Alan, Amy, Vicky." Repeating the words several times, she gradually got louder, then the words changed. "Ester and Joseph. Ester and Joseph." Again, with each chant, her voice became louder and stronger. She was getting into the zone. No longer did she care what the neighbours thought, and all worries of Alan and his potential affair had now been banished. Alice, Jack and John came next, repeated several times, quickly followed by Sabine.

Something was happening to Rose, something that she didn't understand and had no control over. Her body felt as though it was on fire as she sat rocking to-and-fro in the old chair, shouting at the top of her voice. It was cathartic. Eventually her chants quietened, and her shoulders dropped. The chair stopped rocking and she fell silent with her head flopped forward.

The smell, that same sweet earthy aroma of hay and raisins, began to fill her nostrils as a vision appeared in her mind's eye. The old man. He was here in the garden with her smoking a pipe. That was the smell. Pipe tobacco. An unearthly howl in the near distance startled her, suddenly jolting her back.

"What was that? What's happening?"

Confused, she tried to stand, but her legs were weak and wobbly, causing her to steady herself on the chair arm and lower herself gently back down. "Where am I?" a quiet whisper, falling from her lips as she came to her senses. Surprised, she opened her eyes wide and stared. The garden was bathed in a luminous white light. The moon. The full moon was shining down, cloaking everything in a silvery sheen, while fallen leaves whipped about her in the stiff breeze. It felt truly magical.

"I've done it, I've done it," she whispered, trying to recall the image of the old man smoking his pipe.

Closing her eyes once more, she leaned back into the old chair, willing the scene to come back. Taking slow steady breaths, she eventually recreated the image as though it was a faded watercolour painted on the inside of her eyelids. "Oh, how I wish I could paint."

A brown flat cap, perched on a bald head, topped a creased and weather worn face with an old clay pipe between its pursed lips. His tired green eyes had lost their sparkle, more jade than emerald, but Rose knew in her heart that he was a good man. A tatty, collarless shirt, open at the neck with half-rolled up sleeves, revealed gnarled hands, the texture of leather. Woollen, brown trousers that bagged at the knees, wrinkled around worn, laced up boots. In his left hand was a tool of some sort. A rake perhaps? Rose couldn't be sure. Concentrating hard, she looked at his left hand curled around the shaft of his rake. It was missing a finger. Screwing her eyes even tighter she stared harder. Yes, his little finger on his left hand was definitely missing. 'Gosh! I wonder how he lost that.'

Another howl, nearer this time, forced Rose to open her eyes. Then she heard something jump behind her. Slowly turning, she saw a fox climbing over the fence into the garden. Frozen to her chair, she held her breath and stared in awe as it sauntered past her as if she wasn't there, turned the corner, and continued down the drive out of sight.

'Nellie! Where's Nellie?'

Beginning to panic, Rose looked around her for her faithful companion. Where was she? Standing abruptly caused another head rush but Rose pushed through it and entered the cottage through the patio doors to find Nellie asleep in her basket by the fire. Relieved, she flopped into a chair to recover.

Suddenly, Edward announced the hour, it was midnight. What had just happened?

9.

Sunday morning dawned cold and foggy and Rose had a headache to match the weather. Needing to clear her mind, she stepped under a cool, refreshing shower and made a cup of peppermint tea. By mid-morning, the fog had lifted, taking her malaise along with it. Glancing out of the window, her eyes landed on the crystal ball still resting on the patio table. It needed to be brought back inside before Alan returned. The next thing to catch her attention was the rocking chair, draped with a bottle green throw. The blanket ought to come in to be aired and the chair should be placed in the shed to protect it from the worst of the winter weather still to come. Wondering just how she was going to manage that task on her own, her mind drifted to last night. Memories came flooding back, along with the feeling that she'd had no control over her thoughts and actions. Just what had happened? Had she conjured up the image of the old man in her imagination or was it truly witchcraft? Was she really a proper witch now? About to go outside, she was stopped in her tracks by chimes from the front doorbell. Pausing, she tried to recall her engagements for the week ahead. No, she wasn't expecting anybody; Alan wouldn't be back until late afternoon and he had a key. Puzzled, she opened the door to discover Freya stood on the step.

"Oh, hi, I, erm, didn't know you were coming."

"I didn't know I was coming either until my bike drew me down your drive."

Once inside the two women embraced and went in the kitchen for coffee.

Freya smiled at her friend, sensing a subtle change in her energy. "So, how did it go last night?"

Sucking in her lips and cocking her head to one side Rose paused, searching for the right words. "I'm not sure really."

Disappointed, Freya continued her questions. "Well, was it a good – I'm not sure, or a bad – I'm not sure?"

"Good, I think."

"Well, that's positive. So tell me, what happened?"

Lifting her cup to her lips, Rose took a sip of the hot, bitter liquid and shrugged. "I don't know where to begin."

"The beginning is always a good place. Start from the moment you got out of bed yesterday. I want to know everything."

An hour later, Rose had recounted the whole story to Freya, from waving Alan away early in the morning to climbing into bed exhausted after midnight.

Leaning forward, Freya squeezed her friend on the

shoulder. "I'm thrilled for you Rose, you're getting there."

Unsure of where 'there' really was, Rose turned to glance out of the window. "Oh, while you're here, will you help me to carry the old chair into the shed? It can't stay out all winter."

"We can do better than that. Let's bring it back inside where it belongs."

"Mm, but Alan wasn't happy with it in the dining room..."

Freya knew that she'd have to choose her words carefully and not just blurt out what she was thinking. "This is your home Rose, as well as Alan's. Where would you like it?"

Surprised by her friends' comments, Rose stood and walked to the window. Freya was right. She needed to stand her ground occasionally, like she had with the pond. She'd won that battle, hadn't she? The word 'battle' rattled about in her head. Was her marriage becoming a battle ground? Trying to push that thought aside, she sighed and looked back at the tatty old chair. Alan did have a point, it was past its best, but it did belong here. She wasn't sure how she knew, but she was certain of that now.

"Do you have a spare room?"

"Yes, but there's not much space left."

"Show me."

Leading the way, Rose took Freya down the corridor to the spare room and invited her inside. It was simply furnished with twin beds, a built-in wardrobe, a small chest of drawers sitting under the window with a basket chair in the corner.

"This is a lovely room; does it face North?" Rose shrugged, never having thought about it before. Undeterred, Freya picked up the basket chair, continuing with her quest. "Do you have somewhere else you can put this? Then the rocking chair could go here. It would be a great space to help you transcend from the physical realm."

Deciding to let Freya take charge, Rose put the small chair in the study and the two women carried the old rocking chair inside from the back garden, placing it in the corner of the spare room next to the window.

"There, that's better. Back where it belongs – well almost." Puzzled by the last comment Rose looked up questioningly, but Freya cut her off. "Gosh, is that the time? I'd better be on my way."

Once Freya had left, Rose replayed their meeting in her head. What did she mean by, 'You're getting there'? Why did it matter which way the spare room faced and what was she supposed to transcend into? So many questions. Freya hadn't explained anything to her about last night's bizarre experience. And she hadn't mentioned her own full moon event either, despite her asking several times. It seemed that Freya had an uncanny knack of changing the subject back onto Rose. But why? Ruminating, she tidied the rest of her things away and continued with her chores.

Just as expected, Alan returned later in the day to find no trace of Rose's full moon ceremony, greeting her with his predictable peck on the cheek before turning the TV on to catch the weekend's Grand Prix.

With Alan now back at work, Rose decided it was time to sort out some cushions for the old rocking chair. First, she measured the seat and back, noticing even more green paint splashed on its mismatched spindles. A quick trip out to the workshop equipped her with a sheet of sandpaper, perhaps that would get it off. Using all of her strength she began to rub the spindles, but this caused the chair to rock. An idea popped into her head, if she laid it on its side, it would stay still. It worked. Kneeling down she began rubbing, getting most of the splashes off. Pleased with herself she pushed her glasses back up her nose, bringing the underneath of the seat into focus. What was that mark? Squinting, she leaned closer. Initials. Somebody's initials were engraved into the wood. But what did it say? It was quite difficult to read. The first letter was B, but what was the other one? Tracing it with a fingernail, she tried to picture what it said, but failed. Frustrated, she stood pondering what to do next. Of course, her phone. She quickly grabbed it and snapped a photo then stretched the screen to enlarge it. B M. The initials were B M. And there was a date. Eighteen- fifty-four. Wow! The chair really was old. Pleased with herself, she did a little happy dance around it. But her euphoria didn't last long before the next question popped into her head. Who was B M?

The rest of the morning was spent trawling through the old photos and documents that had been left in a box in the kitchen when they'd first arrived. There were old photographs of the cottage going back through the years, but none of them contained people. A couple were aerial shots that had clearly once been hung on a wall. Others were of a previous pine kitchen when it had been newly installed. One was a photo of a brick fireplace in the study that was no longer there. Frustrated, she turned to the previous property deeds that had been collected over the years. The old cottage had swapped owners many times, and there was a pile to get through. The most recent one was six years ago and the earliest one was dated nineteen-nineteen. It had previously been part of a large country estate and the landowner had sold it to a woman, a sitting tenant, for two hundred pounds, but her initials weren't B M. How could she find out the identity of B M?

Alongside the deeds were sets of drawings and a planning application for the latest extension that was now their bedroom and ensuite. As interesting as it was,

THE WITCH'S CHAIR

Rose was no nearer to finding her mysterious stranger who had presumably made the rocking chair. Beyond frustrated, she tidied the things away and drove into town to source fabric to make cushions for the chair. It deserved a new lease of life.

10.

The small market town was several miles away. Armed with her measurements, Rose trawled through the shops on the high street but didn't find any selling fabrics. Next, she scoured the market, but most of the stalls were selling fruit and veg, cards, clothes, pet supplies or toiletries. Now what? An image of her friend popped into her head. The charity shops. Of course, Freya had said to look in the charity shops. With renewed enthusiasm she marched around the outside of the stalls and continued her search. The first shop she found was for a cancer charity; she didn't find any fabric but came out with a rustic looking butter dish that she felt would work better in her cottage kitchen rather than the modern dish they currently used.

Her next stop was a shop supporting homeless people where she bought an earthenware bowl that spoke to her. After that it was an outlet for a hospice, followed by one collecting for stray animals. Rose hadn't been in many charity shops previously and was fascinated by the items on display. Who had they previously belonged to and how did they end up here? It was clear that some of the trinkets were quite old and had possibly belonged to people who were no longer alive. House clearances perhaps, someone's treasured possessions. The memory of disposing of her dear mother's items after she'd passed away last year caused her to pause for a moment; that had been a particularly difficult time, deciding what to keep and what to let go. Yes, Freya was right, she mused. Nothing truly belonged to us. These pieces were merely clutter to comfort us in our mortal life. Life! Was there really life after death?

Now oblivious to her surroundings Rose startled when a middle-aged lady approached her with a cheery smile. "Can I help you?"

"Oh, I'm sorry, I was miles away." Producing a piece of paper from her pocket Rose continued, "I'm looking for some fabric to make a couple of cushions for an old chair."

Glancing around the interior of the dingy shop the lady rubbed her chin, "Mm, we don't get much in the way of fabric, but we do have a good collection of curtains. You could probably fashion some cushions out of them. What colour had you got in mind?"

Another decision. When had she become so dithery and indecisive? She felt sure that she'd hadn't always been like this. The menopause. Perhaps that had something to do with it.

"I'm not sure, I haven't given it much thought."

"Well, why don't you go and have a look, something might catch your eye."

Rose instantly picked out a pair of old curtains that

appealed to her. They had a sage green background and were covered with birds and berries. Perfect. A trip to a craft shop for zips, thread and filling completed her outing and she drove home contented.

Sewing didn't come naturally to Rose, the odd button or repair she could manage, but she persevered and by the evening of the following day she had completed her task. Pleased with herself, she secured the cushions in place and stood back to admire her work. Perfect. As an afterthought, she took a quick picture and sent it to Freya. Her friend replied swiftly.

Wow! Rose, that's amazing. Very Arts and Crafts. Well done.

Her next thought was to call Alan in to admire her handywork, but she decided that probably wasn't the best idea. He hadn't even noticed that the rocking chair was back inside the house, and she wasn't prepared to have it consigned to the shed or worse. No, she decided to keep quiet, not wanting another battle on her hands.

Wednesday morning came around and again she found herself at a meeting. This time it was at Scarlet's house. All of the members were present, and most of them were now wearing dark velvet dresses and woolly tights with the colder weather making floaty summer dresses impractical. Glancing down at her dull brown trousers and sensible shoes, Rose felt somewhat underdressed. There had never been a mention of a uniform or dress code, well, not while she'd been present, and Freya was dressed in a similar fashion to herself, warm and sensible. While Shona set about opening the meeting, Rose found herself deep in thought. Should she look online for a velvet dress, or even a cloak? Alan would think she'd taken leave of her senses if he ever found it.

"So, let's start with Rose."

Somewhere, in the periphery of her consciousness, she felt sure someone had said her name. Snapping her head up, she gazed about the room. All eyes were on her. Clueless, she glanced across to Freya for help. She didn't fail her.

"I think Rose may be a little unsure of her talent and ability yet, it's still early days for her. She did, however, share the events of her full moon ritual with me, perhaps I could relay it to you. With Rose's permission, of course."

Mortified, Rose managed a smile and a nod, wondering what on earth Freya might disclose. Did she want this group of strangers to know her raw, intimate details? Her full moon experience felt personal and private. She still had no idea herself what had really happened. Perhaps she shouldn't have joined a group after all, she was never comfortable when in the spotlight. But then she wouldn't have met Freya.

"Great idea Freya. Thank you." Shona then smiled at Rose before continuing. "It can take a while to feel confident when entering a new form of spirituality. We all have to begin somewhere."

Freya squared her shoulders and sat tall. "I bumped into Rose completely by chance the following morning and she told me that her first attempt, in her front garden felt unnatural and uncomfortable, so she retreated to her back garden, placed her crystals on her altar and sat staring into a bowl of rainwater." Freya looked over to Rose and winked, then continued, "Apparently it was slow to begin with, but eventually the moon made an appearance and Rose felt herself slip into a trance like state. Have I got that right Rose?"

Rose nodded and found her voice, "Yes, that's correct; then I thought I saw an image of someone, but I don't know who."

Eager eyes were now upon her, and one member asked, "What happened next?"

Unsure of a suitable response she faltered, and Freya jumped in, "A fox howling in the adjacent woods broke her trance."

Shona was the next to speak. "Well done, and thank you for sharing. Alison, why don't you go next?"

Alison's account was long and drawn out, detailing the herbs and crystals that she'd used and the incense that she'd burned while sat staring into her wonderful firepit alongside her perfect family. Rose wiped the palms of her hands down her trousers and felt the sweat trickle down her brow, wondering if she dared to remove her jumper. The meeting seemed to drag on and she was now doubting her motives; she didn't belong in this group. But she knew she needed Freya's wisdom. She was fast becoming a true friend and mentor.

Freya was the first to leave and Rose quickly followed her out onto the drive.

"Thank you for saving me, I owe you. Let me buy you lunch."

"You don't need to repay me Rose, I could see you were a little uncomfortable."

"Definitely. I'm not sure this witch thing is for me."

Turning abruptly, Freya's vivid green eyes widened and she took hold of Rose's wrist. "Oh, it most certainly is, but you don't have to be in a group."

Frowning, Rose stopped. "What do you mean? Aren't witches supposed to belong to a coven or something?"

"Witches can be whatever they want, as long as they do no harm. I'm more of a solitary witch myself, but I come along to the meetings for companionship. Living alone can be a bit lonely at times." A silent pause followed which made Rose feel a little uncomfortable. Sensing the awkwardness Freya continued, "I made a big pan full of soup yesterday; there's plenty left. Come to mine, but you'll have to drive slowly. I'll follow you on my bike."

"I've got a loaf in the bread maker; it will be ready now. I'll nip and get it then meet you at yours."

When Rose arrived, Freya was busy in the kitchen. The two women shared a simple lunch then retreated to sit in front of the open fire in the cosy lounge. There was no need for words while they relaxed and gazed into the dancing flames. It felt magical. Rose could feel her energy and confidence growing. It felt comforting as though there was something glowing deep inside her.

Pleased with her incantation and the special ingredient that she'd added to the soup, Freya sat back and enjoyed watching Rose's aura manifest. It began gradually, turning from the barely perceptible, dull, smudged grey that she usually wore to a pale lilac. With time, it intensified in small increments, gaining more colour and vitality until it eventually settled at a gentle shade of lavender. Freya already knew that Rose had the ability hidden somewhere inside her soul, obscured beneath years of caring for her family. Her children, elderly parents and husband had all taken their toll, but it wasn't too late, her psychic ability was still alive. All she had to do was nurture it and it would return. But the spell wouldn't last for long, perhaps long enough for Rose to feel it and work on building its strength for herself. How should she tell her? Freya knew that she couldn't impose this information onto her friend. No,

Rose needed to work it out for herself. There were ways though. Freya thought that she might be able to help her friend without her knowing. She'd try to send her healing energy. She was aware that a close bond was flourishing between them, more than friendship. Something stronger, something had drawn them together as though it was meant to be. Freya realised that she needed to be patient and the reason would eventually materialise. With patience and resolve, all would eventually become clear.

11.

Christmas was fast approaching and Vicky, Rose's youngest daughter, arrived for the weekend. Alan kept himself busy in his mancave while mother and daughter hit the shops. They visited Rose's favourite garden centre for lunch where she told her daughter about the initials and date on the old chair.

Vicky was fascinated. "I have a friend who's always on an ancestry website. She's tracked her family way back to the seventeenth century. I'll send her a message to see if she can help find your mystery person."

When they reached home, Vicky had the information she needed to begin the search.

"You need to subscribe to the website then you'll be ready to go."

"But you know I'm hopeless with computers Vicky; I always mess it up and have to ask your dad to help me. Then he gets grumpy."

"Come on Mum, I'll show you how to log on and put a link on your screen. You'll get the hang of it."

By the time Vicky went home, Rose had managed to navigate the website and felt confident to have a go on her own. It was very slow work, with only initials and a date to work with, so far leading to a dead end. But she vowed to persevere. She'd managed to track the people who had lived and worked in the cottage as far as nineteen-nineteen but then the trail went cold, the occupants prior to that had all been tenants, probably farmers. And it hadn't been called Orchard Cottage back then either, it had simply been The Bothy on an old map of the village. Frustrated, she rubbed her eyes, closed her laptop, and made a hot chocolate. It was bedtime. But just who was B M? And what was the significance?

Pouring rain woke Rose early the following morning, Alan was still asleep, so she crept into the kitchen to make tea. At seven-thirty she prepared a breakfast tray and took it into him, having performed an incantation earlier to try to salvage their failing marriage.

"What time is it? Am I late?"

"No darling, you're never late. I just thought I'd treat you this morning."

Puzzled, Alan sat up wondering what the occasion was; he'd already had his birthday. Rose had been acting out of character recently, he mused. He couldn't quite put his finger on it, but she'd been quiet, almost secretive. And assertive at times, quite unlike her.

Rose's words drifted into his head. "It's tipping it down."

"Yes, apparently it's going to turn to snow later. What are your plans for today?"

"Oh, you know, just the usual jobs."

She knew she couldn't tell him what she really had planned for today; she was trawling through the old parish records on the internet again for a man, with the initials B M who had lived in The Bothy in eighteen-fifty-four, hoping she'd have more success this time.

Once Alan had left, she made herself cosy in the study and began her search. The old parish council records were handwritten and very difficult to read. The words had been scribed in ink and were often smudged and the writing was cursive and very slanted, making the task arduous. It was easy to track back to nineteen-twenty but prior to that it belonged to the landed gentry, as had most of the old village and the trail went cold. Frustrated, she sighed and leaned back in her chair. What was that patch near the top of the wall? Carefully climbing onto the chair, she reached up to investigate. Damp. It was an area of damp where the wall met the ceiling. Had it been there when they'd bought the cottage? Rose didn't think so. They'd had a structural survey done and she felt sure it wasn't mentioned on that. Unsure what to do, she took a photo of it and sent it to Alan. Normally she didn't contact him at work unless it was urgent, but she felt sure he'd want to know. An hour later he sent her a reply.

Can you find a builder and get them to come out and investigate?

Really? He wanted her to deal with it. What did she know about builders? Suddenly an idea popped into her head. Jim who'd dug the hole for her pond. Yes, she'd ring Jim. Another hour passed before he responded to her voicemail.

Not fit to turn a cat out in this rain. I'll call round in the morning if it's fine.

Thankfully, the day dawned bright and clear with a heavy frost. Jim arrived at lunchtime and proceeded to climb up onto the roof. By the time he reappeared Rose was waiting with a steaming mug of strong, sweet tea.

"What's the verdict?"

Scratching his head, Jim sucked in a long breath. "It's yonder chimney. Got a nasty crack in it. Needs to come down."

"Oh, which one, there are four."

"That one there. Do yer use it?"

Rose craned her neck to work out which chimney he was pointing to. "No, no we don't. There isn't a fireplace for that one anymore."

"Best take it down then. Won't be cheap ya know."

"Nothing ever is Jim. When can you do it?"

"I finish for Christmas next week. It'll be new year, if it

stays dry."

Rose sent Alan an update; all they could do was wait and hope for good weather, but it was winter.

Predictably the weather wasn't kind, but Rose carried on with her Christmas preparations the best she could. The circle meetings were paused for the festive season, but Rose was determined to celebrate the shortest day of the year. December the twenty-first. The winter solstice. Somehow it now appeared more significant to her than Christmas day, but she couldn't explain that to Alan. No, she'd have to find a way to celebrate in secret. But how? She'd finished her Christmas shopping; the turkey was in the freezer and the girls would be arriving on Christmas Eve; Amy was bringing Tom and Rose was looking forward to being a family again. The presents were wrapped and under the tree, but she needed to visit Freya to take her present. She'd found the perfect gift, in fact, it was so nice that she'd also bought herself one. It was a knee length kimono in black with a very witchy pattern printed on it. Bones, frogs, bats and rats. She'd found it online at a website called 'Cosmic Drifters'. With time running out she rang her friend.

"I'd love to see you Rose, why don't you come on the twenty-first? I'll make a simple supper."

"But that's the solstice!"

"Exactly, the very moment when the world balances on a knife edge between the dark and the light. We can celebrate the restoration of the light together."

On the twenty-first, Alan looked back at his wife somewhat perplexed. "How do you mean you won't be in for supper?"

"I've been invited to a friend's house. All you need to do is put your plate in the microwave for five minutes. It's simple, even you can manage that."

Once Rose had left, Alan sat down. He was truly speechless. She never went out in the evenings. Who was this friend, he wondered? She hadn't mentioned anybody before, apart from Betty at the café. Perhaps she'd gone there, but why would she? The ping from the microwave announced that his dinner was ready, warmed up chilli, the leftovers from yesterday. With his appetite now gone, he leaned against the breakfast bar. A disturbing thought wormed its way into his head. Was she seeing another man? She had seemed strange for a few months now. Was she unhappy? Didn't she love him anymore? Insecurity was an unfamiliar sensation to Alan and he didn't like it. In fact, he thought, it felt like a rock in the pit of his stomach.

Food was unimportant now. He logged into their bank statement. Nothing seemed to be amiss, no hotel bookings or unusual activity. There were transactions from several online shops, but it was Christmas so they would probably be presents for the girls. Yes, 'Cosmic Drifters' sounded like a modern, girly place where she might get something for one of their daughters. His mind wandered further. He hadn't bought Rose a present yet and there were only a few days left. He'd have to pop into town tomorrow, but what could he get her?

12.

Stepping into Freya's house was almost an overload of the senses for Rose. She didn't know where to look first. It was like walking into a forest, the smell of pine jostling with the aromas of seasonal spices wafting in from the kitchen, ginger, nutmeg, cloves and cinnamon, all wrestling for her attention. Festooning the walls of the tiny cottage were holly, ivy, mistletoe and pine foliage. The fire was roaring, filling the room with an ambient glow. It was absolutely perfect.

"Wow!"

Studying her guest, Freya noticed that her aura had dimmed again. "Welcome Rose, let me take your coat."

Once seated Rose's eyes continued surveying the space. "It's amazing, where did you get all of this from?"

"The ivy is from my garden, but the rest is foraged, with the permission of the plants of course."

A worrying thought crossed Rose's mind. Did the person who chopped her Christmas tree down seek its permission first? She rather thought not. Freya's idea was much better; she hadn't killed anything, just taken a little greenery and left the plants unharmed to regrow. Feeling guilty, Rose tried to focus on something else, her gift.

"This is just a small gift; I hope you like it."

As Freya carefully removed the wrapping paper, Rose began to doubt her choice. It was obvious now that Freya would have much preferred something natural like a beeswax candle or a houseplant.

"Oh Rose, it's lovely. Thank you."

After carefully folding the wrapping paper to repurpose later, Freya put her new kimono on, while Rose rummaged in her bag and found hers and slid her arms into the garment.

"There, now we're twins."

The two women hugged then Freya produced a small, parcel wrapped in brown paper, tied with string.

"This is for you Rose."

As carefully as she could, Rose opened the present to reveal a small brown glass bottle. She took the lid off and inhaled deeply, expecting it to be a sweet-smelling aromatherapy mix. She was wrong. It smelled of decomposing vegetation.

Trying to hide her embarrassment she frowned and coughed. "Huh, sorry. Not quite what I expected. What is it for?"

Amused, Freya took the bottle from her and replaced the lid. "It's a tincture that I've prepared for you. It's very concentrated; you only need to add two drops to some warm water. You'll barely be able to taste it."

Rose wasn't convinced, and Freya hadn't told her what it was a remedy for. She wasn't aware that she had any health issues, apart from the pesky menopause.

"Is it for my hot flushes?" she questioned.

"No, it's to help you on your journey."

Frowning, Rose was even more puzzled now. "What journey? We haven't booked our holidays yet."

Trying hard not to laugh, Freya knew she was going to have to spell it out. "Your spiritual journey Rose. You've got so much ability deep within you, but you need to gently coax it out."

Freya went into the kitchen and came back with two teacups full of a steaming liquid. She gave one to her friend. "Here, let me add two drops to this."

Cautiously, Rose sniffed the golden liquid. "Ooh, is it punch?"

"Not quite, it's wassail." Once again Rose frowned questioningly and Freya continued, "It's hot cider infused with spices and fruit. You won't even notice the tincture."

She was right. "Mm, delicious, but I'm driving. I'll only have a sip."

Sitting back in the squishy leather sofa, nursing her drink, Rose sighed as she began to relax. She felt at home, comfortable and content. She continued to gaze into the flames while her friend busied herself in the kitchen.

When Freya popped her head through the adjoining door to announce that supper was ready, she immediately noticed the violet light surrounding Rose. It was working. The two women shared a vegetable casserole followed by traditional homemade figgy pudding. Freya had set out an extra dish containing a small helping of the festive fayre.

Curiosity got the better of Rose. "Were you expecting another guest?"

"No, that's the offering to the sun. We'll need it later."

Back in front of the fire with another cup of Wassail in hand, Rose decided it was time to learn more about Freya. She wasn't going to let her diversionary tactics prevent her this time.

"So, you know everything about me. I want to hear your story."

"There isn't much to tell, and it's nearly time for our ritual."

Relieved, Freya went about collecting the required items and took them out into her neat courtyard, then she came back with a large copper pan and carefully picked a burning log out of the fire.

"You'll need your coat, it's snowing."

When Rose entered the space, she was blown away. The small fire burning in the bottom of the pan was placed in the centre of a circle which was formed out of pebbles, shells and twigs. Unsure of what she was supposed to do she looked at her friend.

"Just relax and do whatever comes naturally."

First, Freya lit a bundle of sage and wafted the smoke over Rose and herself. Rose was familiar with this; it was to cleanse and purify. Next, Freya walked clockwise around the circle with the sage while chanting. Then she took Rose's hand and guided her into the centre where both women stood looking towards the sky. Snow was now falling thick and fast, gradually smothering their hair and clothing. It felt surreal. Taking hold of both of her hands Freya turned to Rose and closed her eyes. Rose followed suit. Then it began.

"We welcome the all-knowing this yuletide eve to our midwinter reflection ritual. We invite you to join our circle. Lend us your stamina and bestow your blessings upon us. Thank you for the restoration of the light."

Freya then looked at Rose and nodded, prompting her to repeat the chant. Next, she placed a smooth pink pebble in Rose's left hand and turned to face the small fire. Freya passed her left hand over the top of the pan of fire and urged her friend to do the same. The two women then fell silent, watching the snow fall onto the ground as it slowly extinguished the dying embers. Several minutes later, Freya removed a stick from the circle as though she were opening a gate.

"I open this circle and gratefully return its energy back into our Mother Earth, knowing the light will surely return."

Next, Freya took the small bowl of food and placed it on the low stone wall. "Thank you, Lord and Lady, for your presence tonight."

The two women beamed at each other, shook the snow out of their hair and ran back inside the kitchen where Freya handed Rose a hot toddy.

"I can't drink this; I need to drive home."

"You won't be driving anywhere tonight in this weather Rose; you'll have to stay over."

Striding over to the small lounge window Rose peered out onto the road. It was silent and still. A true silent night. Concerned, she found her phone. It had several missed calls from Alan. Poor Alan. She hadn't given him a thought since she'd left home. Had he managed to warm his supper? He would be worried about her by now. Hurriedly, she called him. He wasn't happy.

"Can't you come and get me in the Stelvio?"

Freya couldn't hear his response, but she concluded it was negative.

"But it's four-wheel drive..."

Another silence followed.

"Okay. Yes, I'll be fine. I'll ring you in the morning. Bye."

Sighing, Rose shrugged. "Sorry, he's had a couple of glasses of wine and can't drive either. I could call for a taxi."

"You'll do no such thing. You're staying and that's final. Now you can drink as much as you like."

Sipping her drink cautiously, in case it had something foul tasting added, Rose sighed; it was very pleasant, warming and comforting after being out in the snow.

As if reading her mind, Freya interrupted her thoughts. "It's whisky and green ginger wine."

She wasn't a big drinker and Rose knew she shouldn't have anymore. Then another thought disturbed her. Where would she sleep? She felt sure that there was only one bedroom. Flopping down onto the squishy sofa, her mind was made up; she'd sleep downstairs on the sofa. It was cosy and warm in front of the fire. Yes, she'd sleep like a log.

While the two women gazed into the flames in companiable silence, Rose knew she'd got her friend captive. Somehow, she would delve into Freya's past. She'd have to be discreet, no direct questions, but she was determined.

"This is such a lovely cottage, how old is it?"

Freya's features softened and she smiled at her friend. "It was built in the eighteen-fifties. It's an old railway cottage."

Rose's head snapped up. "What a coincidence! The rocking chair was made about the same time, eighteen-fifty-four to be precise."

"Wow! How did you find that out?"

"Oh, it's engraved underneath the seat with an initial. B M. Didn't I tell you?"

"Nope, I would have remembered that."

"Sorry, so much going on with Christmas and the leaking roof at the moment."

"So, have you found out who B M is?"

"Sadly not, but I'm on to it."

A short while later, Rose had explained about trawling through the parish council records without any success.

Stifling a yawn Freya stood up. "Come on, time for bed."

"Oh, I'll sleep here on the sofa…"

"Nonsense, I've got a double bed. You'll sleep much better upstairs."

Unable to persuade Freya otherwise, Rose reluctantly used the bathroom, where she removed her clothes but wrapped her kimono tightly around herself. Freya was already in bed and Rose gently slid in beside her, laying rigid.

"Relax Rose, sleep well."

In no time Freya's breathing changed and Rose knew she was asleep. But sleep was nowhere to be found for Rose. It wasn't that unusual. Alan always dropped off quickly and she often laid awake listening to him snoring. But it wasn't snoring that was causing her discomfort at the moment. No, it was Freya. Was she a lesbian? Rose didn't mind if she was, she had no issues with homosexuality, but she feared that she might just be coming on to her. Still feeling uncomfortable, she took her pillow and a soft throw and crept downstairs. Yes, she'd be far more comfortable on the sofa tonight.

An hour later and she was still wide awake. This was going to be awkward; she wanted to be friends with Freya, just not in that way. What should she say? Rose tried to relax and gazed into the dying embers and eventually her eyelids drooped.

"It's a little girl Anne, come on, wake up! You have a

daughter."

The old woman placed the baby in the wooden box and covered it with a shawl. She knew her task wasn't over; the girl had lost too much blood. Attempting to stem the flow, she pressed rags between her limp legs. It was no use.

"Call for Dr James, we're losing her!"

A slim woman ran from the house, clutching her coat, to raise the alarm.

The frail baby stirred and made a pitiful cat like mewl.

"Get yerself in 'ere lad and take care o' the bairn, we can't lose her as well."

The ginger-haired man howled, like a wounded fox at the sight that met him. Anne, his beloved wife lay pale and motionless.

The haunting wail of an injured animal woke Freya. Where was Rose? In seconds she was down the stairs at her friend's side. Her skin was flushed and sweat was trickling down her brow.

"Rose, Rose, can you hear me?"

"What? Where am I?"

"It's okay Rose, it's Freya. You're safe now." Freya knew it had been a vision – the tincture had worked, but what had Rose witnessed? She needed to tread carefully. Rose was clearly in a fragile state.

13.

Clear skies and sunshine woke the two friends. Freya had sat next to Rose on the sofa most of the night while she recounted her strange dreams and was now in no doubt about her hidden ability. She was a scryer; she had the power to look into certain mediums to have visions, a true witch. All she had to do now was learn how to control it. She'd need to acquire the skills to interpret what she saw, but it wasn't easy. It took practise and patience. She should know. It had taken Freya years to hone her skills as a medium, to understand the cards and runes. But now she was in no doubt that Rose would get there with a little help.

"I know you will solve your mystery; you just need to keep practising with different media; mirrors, clouds, fires, water, anything that takes your fancy. And keep using the tincture. Two drops every day."

After helping her friend clear the snow from her car she waved, as Rose drove off into the unfamiliar white landscape, with the protection amulet that Freya had insisted she accepted hung around her neck. It had worked. She arrived home safely expecting to meet Alan's wrath. But she was pleasantly surprised.

As soon as he heard the tyres crunching on the frozen snow, he rushed out of the house to greet her with a hug. "Oh, Rose. Thank goodness you're safe. I was worried about you."

It was the first day of his Christmas break from work and she felt sure he would spend most of his time in the garage, but she didn't mind. Her plan was to practise scrying; she'd promised to report back to Freya.

"I'm fine, in fact I had a super time. Did you manage to warm your supper?"

In the kitchen the smell of freshly brewed coffee awaited and she snatched the opportunity to add two drops of the tincture when he was distracted by their dog.

Draining his cup, he took her hand and smiled. "Let's get kitted up and go out for a long walk like we used to. I'll make a flask."

Nellie ran in front of them, scampering about following the tell-tale tracks of small rodent prints in the snow. Alan held tight onto his wife's hand deep in thought. When had they begun to drift apart? Was it his fault? Had he neglected her that much? But he knew the answer. Yes. He'd increasingly spent more and more time with his cars. But what had they in common now? The girls had left, and he was still working full time. Was it too late to rectify his mistakes? A gasp from Rose made him startle. Was she okay?

"Oh! How beautiful."

Turning, he saw Rose making her way over to a frozen pond, the low sunlight glinting off its polished surface, shattering into a myriad of colours. She was right, it was indeed beautiful. Once he reached the edge, he removed his backpack, laid a rug on the hard ground and poured two mugs of cocoa. Joining him, Rose sat silently, staring at the view while sipping her drink. It felt surreal. Special. And it made the hairs on the back of her neck stand on end like a row of soldiers on parade. She knew that this place had magical potential. If only she were by herself. How could she explain anything to her husband? He'd think she'd gone mad. There was no way he would ever understand that there was far more to the world than the things that his eyes could see. Energy and spirits. No, he'd never get his pragmatic head around it. She wasn't even sure that she understood it herself yet!

Following another fresh scent, Nellie ran off towards a group of trees. Alan stood and trudged through the snow after her, leaving Rose alone. This was her chance. Taking several deep breaths, she stared with intent over the shimmering surface, zoning the rest of her surroundings out. Then it happened. It was like a mirage in the desert.

She could see ladders stretched out across its surface with a man crawling across them, the dejected look of resignation on his face. She could taste the fear in his mouth and hear his heart pounding as though it wanted to escape the confines of its bony cage and run while it still had the chance. This was it. What were the odds of him still being alive? Were they going to get John out from under the ice? The tension was almost too much to bear.

A thump on the head made Rose jump out of her skin. What was that? Then she felt the melting snow trickle down her neck. A snowball. Alan had thrown a snowball at her! Under normal circumstances she would have been thrilled and retaliated. But this wasn't normal. In fact, Rose pondered, would anything ever be normal again?

"Sorry, I was throwing it for Nellie. I'm not a very good shot. Are you okay?"

Standing on two legs on the slippery surface was challenging and she stumbled; the dizzy spell didn't help. Alan rushed to her side and saved her from falling.

"I didn't throw it that hard."

A throbbing sensation began in her left temple, and she knew she'd get a migraine. Freya had warned her to try to minimize disruptions when she was scrying, or it could take its toll. Now she'd never know if they got John out alive. Poor Alice. How do you cope with the loss of a child? She could only imagine.

"Give me a minute."

Bending down, Alan gathered their possessions

together and they silently made their way home. One feeling guilty for hitting his wife with a snowball and the other irritated by her husband's ill-timed interruption.

Christmas came and went. Rose enjoyed the brief time spent with their daughters; even Alan had tried to make himself useful, helping with the dishes. She'd been disappointed though when she'd opened her present from him, a new food processor. She knew hers was quite old, but it wasn't the sort of gift she'd imagined. Why couldn't he choose something personal or pretty? It had always been the same. They celebrated the New Year quietly together with a bottle of wine, managing to stay up to watch Big Ben and the fireworks. Alan even suggested another long walk on New Year's Day, but it wasn't the same; the earth had thawed, leaving a quagmire behind.

Eventually, Alan returned to work, freeing up some time for Rose to practise scrying, and she knew exactly where she was going, the pond that they'd visited before Christmas. But would she be able to find it again on her own? She needn't have worried; it seemed that Nellie had remembered the way. Even without the ice on its surface, it was still beautiful, fringed by tall grasses, now brown and withered. No doubt it would be enchanting in spring and summer. It had become her new favourite place. It was a fairly small pond and Rose decided to treat it like opening a circle. First, she walked around its perimeter in a clockwise direction while asking its permission to use its surface for scrying. Then she got her rug out and sat cross-legged in exactly the same spot with Nellie by her side. Trying to picture an image of her friend, she thought back to their winter solstice ritual. 'Do whatever comes naturally.' That's what Freya had said. Suddenly a song popped into her head. It was an old song that she remembered singing when she was a small child at infant school. Could she remember the words? Gulping a lungful of the cold air, she opened her mouth and sang.

Glad that I live am I, that the sky is blue,

Glad for the country lanes, and the fall of dew,

After the sun the rain, after the rain the sun,

This is the way of life, since the world begun.

Yes, she'd remembered it, but was there a second verse? She felt sure there was, but it wouldn't come, so she repeated the first verse twice at the top of her voice. It felt amazing, invigorating, as though she'd been charged with a special energy. It was time. Would she be able to go back to where she'd left off? Closing her eyes, she summoned up the image of the brave man crawling across the ladders on the frozen surface. It wasn't Jack or Albert, he looked like a professional and was wearing an inflated life jacket and a bright yellow hard hat. Rose decided he must be a fireman. It was a static image, one that she'd remembered. But how could she bring him back to life? The tincture. Of course. She'd had two drops in her coffee this morning.

Would it harm if she had some more? Taking the small glass bottle out of her pocket she sighed. It wasn't going to be pleasant; she'd got nothing to dilute it with. Resigned, she held her nose and dribbled a small amount on her tongue. It was truly vile, but she swallowed it anyway. Would it work? There was only one way to find out.

Slowly, the man became animated and continued his arduous crawl across the frozen lake. Rose noticed he was pulling a small inflatable dingy behind him. Before long she heard the sound of the ice creaking and the man stopped, frozen to the spot, like the very lake itself. But he knew time was of the essence. Cautiously, he reached for the inflatable and dragged himself in. Relief passed momentarily across his taught features before they reset themselves back to fear. Slowly, he pushed his paddle through the half-frozen surface until he reached open water, the exact spot where John had gone under. Seconds later he climbed over the side and slid into the icy depths with a sharp intake of breath.

A whimpering sound somewhere in her periphery broke her concentration; it was Nellie, her faithful companion at her side. She too was staring intently at the surface of the lake, clearly watching something. Could she see the visions too? Without warning, a stinging sensation slammed into Rose, stealing her breath away as the painful feeling of a thousand icy needles pricking her skin spread across the entire surface of her chilled body. Alarmed, she clawed at the earth and reached out to feel the reassuring presence of Nellie at her side. The stinging sensation intensified and she panicked, jumping up and stamping her feet to try and rid herself on the severe pain. Once it had subsided, she glanced back at the lake and was gutted to find that the vision was no more. Disappointed, Rose gently calmed her distressed dog then composed herself and they walked home quietly together.

14.

Life continued and the dark days of January passed slowly, with Rose having little success. She was no nearer to solving the mystery of B M. and she'd had no further visions of John, despite returning to her favourite pond. February eventually arrived with lengthening days and a dry spell. Jim, the builder, had contacted her earlier and was coming to start work on the roof tomorrow. That was a relief as the damp patch in the study was rapidly expanding.

Arriving an hour late the following morning, Jim was soon up on the roof with Charlie, his young apprentice, making a lot of noise, throwing bricks and tiles into the yellow skip residing once more on the drive. When he saw Rose in the front garden, admiring her newly emerged snowdrops, he removed his flat cap, scratched his head and bellowed, "You'd be safer inside, Love!"

Feeling foolish, she retreated indoors and decided to bake; the community café was always grateful for donations. Just as she was putting her muffins in the oven, she heard a crashing noise above her head followed by shouting. A minute later there was a sharp knock on the back door. It was Jim with his cap in his hand.

"Are you alright, Love?"

"Yes, why wouldn't I be? What was that noise, Jim?"

Scratching his head again, he shuffled and gazed at the floor looking uncomfortable. "Erm, chimney's collapsed."

"Oh dear, but weren't you taking it down anyway?"

"Aye lass, but we didn't want it to fall through t'roof."

With the muffins now forgotten, Rose followed Jim into the study to find dust swirling like a mini tornado and a pile of bricks and rubble spilling out through a hole near the bottom of a wall.

Staring through the gloom, Rose was relieved to see that Alan's trophy cabinet was intact, if a little dusty. He wasn't going to be happy. "Oh No! What now?"

Jim began moving the rubble and peered through the hole in the wall just as Charlie arrived looking rather sheepish. "Sorry."

"Well, I never! This is a stud wall and there's a brick fireplace behind it. 'Ere, 'ave a look."

Coughing, Rose knelt down beside Jim. "Wow, it's beautiful. Is it Arts and Crafts? Can you take the wall down?"

Blowing his cheeks out, Jim stepped back and glanced around him. He didn't know what 'Arts and Crafts' were but he thought it sounded expensive. "Well, there dun't seem to be any other damage done in 'ere. That were lucky." Jim ran his hands through his remaining hair and took a step forward, and began tapping the wall. It sounded hollow. "Aye, it in't structural; it could come down, but first we need to fix the hole in t'roof and remove what's left o' chimney stack."

With the two men back up on the roof after another cup of strong, sweet tea, Rose braced herself and went to survey the mess. There was no point informing Alan, she decided. He'd find out when he got home. No, she didn't want to spoil his day. Anyway, he'd probably be in a meeting, or tending to something very important.

As predicted, Alan wasn't impressed. 'What were they thinking?' and 'Bloody idiots!' were among several other expletives to leave his mouth.

Trying to defuse the situation, Rose led him to the damaged wall. "But it was an accident Alan, it wasn't their fault. Anyway, come and look through the hole. Can you see the wonderful fireplace?"

"They should have done a risk assessment and made plans..."

Interrupting him, she tried again. "I think it's Arts and Crafts. It will be amazing once it's restored."

But Alan didn't seem overly interested in the fireplace. He was now inspecting his trophy cabinet. Thankfully, Rose had washed and polished his precious display and it was as good as new. It had taken her most of the day, but she knew leaving it in a dishevelled state wasn't an option.

After breakfast the following morning, Alan issued his predictable peck on the cheek and raised an eyebrow. "I take it I won't be coming home to another disaster this evening?"

"No darling, have a good day."

Jim and Charlie arrived early before Alan had left. On his way out he stopped and spoke to the two men on the drive. Rose had no idea what he'd said but hoped that he wasn't being rude to them. After all, it had been an accident, and they'd discovered the wonderful fireplace that had been concealed for years. What a stroke of luck. It was only partly visible and she couldn't wait for the wall to be removed. But it took nearly a week before Jim and Charlie began the task of taking it down. This time, Rose had cleared the room as much as she could and removed all of Alan's possessions, including the many and varied trophies from his motor sport events, not wanting to risk upsetting him further. He'd wanted to sack the two men and find another builder, and he was in favour of leaving the fireplace behind the wall, but Rose had put her foot down and managed to persuade him otherwise. Fingers crossed they wouldn't let her down.

Slowly, the wall came down to reveal its hidden

treasure. It was indeed a beautiful object. Sadly, she wouldn't be able to have a real fire in it, now that the chimney had been removed, but it was a fantastic period feature. Tracing a finger over the ornately carved dark wood surrounding the artfully placed bricks, she sighed when she came to a broken, jiggered area. "It's such a shame parts of it were damaged when the rubble came down. Would you be able to restore it?"

Jim put his hammer down and thought for a minute. If it was up to him, he'd rip it out and plaster the wall, but he kept that thought to himself.

"You'd be best to get a professional in, Love…"

To everyone's surprise Charlie chirped up, "I can do it. In fact, I'd love to."

Jim's mouth dropped open, "You lad, what do you know about it?"

Gaining in confidence Charlie stood tall and squared his shoulders. "Well, quite a lot really, we've done it in college. In fact, I've got to find a project to do for one of my exams." Now turning towards Rose, he continued, "This would be perfect."

Unsure, Rose felt put on the spot, "Oh, I don't know, Love…"

Beginning to feel a little rejected, Charlie cast his mind back to last night; he'd watched the TV programme 'The

Apprentice' and remembered one of the candidates putting on the fight of his life in order not to be fired. It spurred him on. After all, he too was an apprentice and went to college one day a week. He knew he wasn't as clever as the candidates on TV, but what had he got to lose? "I can do it, I really can. I'd do it at the weekends, and I wouldn't charge you, except for any materials. Please give me a chance."

Sucked in by his pleading eyes, Rose was struggling. She knew Alan wouldn't be happy, but she felt sorry for Charlie. "I'll speak to my husband tonight, and see what he says."

She knew full well that Alan would dismiss the idea as idiocy but at least she hadn't made the decision. She could blame it on him.

Her prediction was correct, Alan did dismiss the idea as insane. "What on earth will that young lad know about restoration? And why do we want a fireplace in the study anyway? You hardly ever go in there."

"Quite a bit apparently. He's at college one day a week studying building, or architecture, or something."

"It won't be architecture, that's for sure..."

"You were once his age, doing structural engineering at college. Someone must have believed in you." Feeling more confident she continued, "And the girls, they had to start somewhere. Look at Amy, she interned for a year on peanuts, but it gave her the opportunity to get where she is today."

Feeling defeated Alan relented, but he had one condition, "Okay, but if he messes it up there's no second chance. I'll have a new wall erected and the fireplace will be hidden again – this time forever."

It felt harsh, even mean, but she agreed to his terms. He was right about one thing though. She didn't use the study very often. It felt uninviting, dark and dismal even, but the fireplace would brighten it up enormously. She could fill the fire space with large pillar candles, like the glossy images of interiors in the expensive magazines she glanced at in the supermarket. Yes, that would look fantastic.

When Jim and Charlie arrived the next morning to finish off, she gave him the good news.

Charlie's face lit up like one of the candles that she'd envisaged, and he looked as though he was about to hug her. She liked him and was glad she'd given him the chance.

"Thank you so much. I promise, you won't regret it. I'll make a start next weekend."

He busied himself taking photos and measurements then made a list of requirements. Rose gave him a hundred pounds to buy the materials and eagerly awaited its restoration.

15.

A text from Freya confirmed that she would be attending the circle meeting on Wednesday morning and Rose arranged to pick her up. When they arrived, Shona took her to one side.

"Rose, are you okay? I was worried when you didn't turn up to the last meeting. You missed the Imbolc ceremony."

Flushing, Rose thought back to that fateful day. "I'm sorry, I'd got the builders in. They were taking a chimney down, and it, well, didn't go quite to plan. I did send you a message."

"Yes, I saw that. Have they finished now?"

"Thankfully the roof is completed, just a bit of restoration work left to do inside." Still wondering if the meetings were a good fit for her, she paused and glanced nervously at the door before changing the subject. "Anyway, it's a full moon again this evening; I'm looking forward to that."

"Yes, it's the snow moon. Just a shame it isn't snowing – that would have been truly magical, wouldn't it?"

Anxiously, Rose glanced over to her friend. Why did she feel so uncomfortable in the company of these women? As always, Freya, came to her rescue, offering to hand out the aromatic tea selection on display. It worked and Shona busied herself distributing moon cookies. Unfortunately, it was pouring down, so they were going to hold their full moon ceremony in Shona's conservatory.

Driving rain lashing at the windows and drumming on the roof threatened to drown out the sound of their leader's voice as she opened the circle with the harsh clash of cymbals. Adding to the cacophony was the irritating whirr of the fancy, rotating fan heaters placed in the corners, somewhat spoiling the ambience. It took Rose back to a childhood holiday, a wet week in Filey in a cold, damp caravan. Six-year-old Rose was now firmly back in nineteen-sixty-nine, remembering her impoverished childhood. It wasn't that her parents didn't love her, she knew that they had, but there just wasn't any spare cash for luxuries after their shopping trip for cigarettes and booze. A smile teased at her lips when the phrase 'disposable income' popped into her head. When had that little nugget been invented? She remembered with sadness how most of their clothes came from the local jumble sale, held once a month in the church hall. She even wore second-hand shoes that were never a perfect fit, either pinching her toes or rubbing the back of her heel causing a painful blister. The following year, nineteen-seventy had been special though. Their landlord had installed a bathroom in the attic, and they no longer had to use the outside toilet that was shared with three other families. And for the first time in her life, she'd had a proper bath with bubbles, not a tepid wash down in the kitchen sink. It had seemed so opulent to young Rose, as if all of her birthdays and Christmases had come at once, very different from the life that she and Alan had created for their beautiful children.

"Thank you, ladies. Next week Bridgit is hosting."

Suddenly snapped out of her childhood and catapulted back into the present, Rose blinked. Was it over? What had she missed? And which of the lovely ladies was Bridgit?

With her coat in her hand, Freya approached her. "It's kind of you to give me a lift Rose, it's no fun cycling in this weather."

Making a dash for the dry interior of the car Rose smiled. "Why don't you come to mine for lunch? I'd love to show you the fireplace."

Once their steaming bowls of curried parsnip soup were empty, Rose escorted Freya into the study where she lit her new pillar candles.

"Oh, Wow! It's fantastic Rose. Do you know how old it is?"

Shaking her head, she let her fingers trail once more over the carved wood, "Charlie, a young local man is going to restore the damaged areas for me, then it will be perfect again."

"It's amazing…"

Turning, Rose observed Freya as her words trailed off and she knelt on the floor in front of the burning candles. Her features softened and heavy lids fell down obscuring her sparkling green eyes. Soon, various expressions fleetingly crossed her face, disturbing its surface, almost like throwing a pebble into a pond causing ripples to radiate out from its centre. It felt surreal. She wanted to ask her what she was doing but knew better than to disturb her friend when she was clearly deep in thought – or something. Curious, Rose waited another five minutes until Freya opened her eyes.

"Are you okay? What were you doing?"

"Yes, I'm fine. Could I have a glass of cold water please?"

Handing her the glass, Rose couldn't contain her excitement. "What did you see?"

"I couldn't see anything, sadly, I don't have visions like you. I just have feelings."

"Oh, what sort of feelings did you have?"

"It's difficult to describe really. Vibrations and auras of those no longer here. I'm sure you'll find out who your mystery person is soon."

When Rose dropped Freya back home it was still raining, and the two women hugged. "Enjoy your full moon ceremony tonight, Rose. I'll think of you."

Shrugging, Rose looked up to the leaden skies. "No chance of seeing her tonight, it's a shame."

"Have your ceremony in the study Rose. You don't need to see the moon – she's still there."

After washing the supper dishes, Alan excused himself for an hour, disappearing into the garage and giving Rose the opportunity she'd been waiting for. She carefully placed her collection of herbs and pebbles on the damaged brick hearth in the study and re-lit the candles. Would she be successful? Would she witness the conclusion to any of her visions tonight? Thinking about the long list she shook her head. Which puzzle did she want to solve the most? Ester and Joseph, John under the ice, Sabine being assaulted, poor Anne and her new-born daughter or the biggest mystery of all – who was B M?

With a sigh, she decided that she'd be grateful for any of them. Closing her eyes, she blew out a long, slow breath and tried to empty her mind. As usual, it wasn't easy and tonight she had the added worry about Alan. What if he came in and caught her practising the craft? Jumping up, she went into the utility room and returned with a soft cloth and a bottle of polish. She'd pretend she was clearing away the dust that seemed to linger in the room. Feeling lighter, she tried again. Nothing came for long enough. Was she doing something wrong? It was, after all, supposed to be a full moon ceremony. Taking a deep breath, she had another attempt remembering how Freya had chanted, welcoming the spirits and deities in.

"Thank you, great Goddess, for your presence tonight as you reach your most powerful, transforming from maiden to mother." Still, nothing seemed to happen, what else could she do? The pebbles. Freya had held one tight and passed it over the flame of the small fire. But which pebble ... and would a candle suffice? Finally, she decided on a weighty reddish, brownish stone with white criss-crossing markings that she'd picked out of the local stream. It had reminded her of a kidney when she'd first spotted it in the shallow water. Clutching it tight in her right hand, hoping to receive some energy or inspiration, she slowly passed it over the candles. Then she waited. Soon the magic began, slowly at first, but it built gradually; she could feel vibrations and see vivid colours. Freya had said something similar earlier and now she understood.

Aware of the rain now lashing against the window, she glanced up at the exact moment that the indigo sky was illuminated by an impressive bolt of white lightning. Rose jumped nervously then tried to think of Freya. It was energy. It was a form of great energy, a resource, and she instinctively knew she had to take the opportunity to tap into it.

Standing, she moved over to the window as the loudest thunderclap she'd ever witnessed rattled on the glass, as if it wanted to gain entry. Intuitively, she opened the window a little way as if inviting it inside. A strong gust of wind rushed past her, blowing her hair and lifting her kimono as though it had a life of its own. Mesmerised, she stood while the garment danced and whirled about her body making the fabric shimmer and shine. Then, as quickly as it had arrived, it suddenly retreated, blowing the window wide open. It left Rose breathless, as though all of the oxygen had been sucked from the room. When she turned back to the fireplace, the candles had been extinguished. Baffled and disorientated she fell to her knees and, a short while later, that's where Alan found her with Nellie, her faithful companion, by her side.

16.

Standing in the doorway he faltered, what was his wife doing on her knees in the study? Closing the distance with long strides he was at her side, grasping her by her arm helping her back onto her feet.

"Rose. Rose, what happened? Are you alright?"

Carefully, he helped her onto the basket chair in the corner, a shiver ran down his spine and he glanced over to the open window where the rain was blowing through and forming a puddle on the window sill. Swiftly closing the window his attention was now back on Rose, his darling wife. Was she ill? Feeling vulnerable he imagined life without her by his side and he didn't like it.

"Rose what happened? Talk to me."

Bewildered, she tried to speak but the words came out more like a croak, as though she had a severe bout of laryngitis. Alan was even more upset now, had she suffered a stroke? Or worse, been struck by the lightening? It had been immensely powerful, that was the reason he'd come back inside as it had taken the power out, he couldn't possibly continue working in the dark.

Taking her face between his hands he tried again, his anxiety now reaching an all-time high.

"Rose, darling, tell me what's happened. Please!"

Tears were now rolling down her cheeks, how could she tell him what had happened when she didn't truly know herself. What would he say if he knew she was a witch? Now frantic he took his phone out of his pocket, "I'm calling for an ambulance!"

"No! Please don't." Her words came out louder now and her voice was regaining some of its strength.

"Well talk to me then, what happened Rose? Why were you on the floor in the study?"

His breathing began to calm, and he took hold of her hand, "Come on, let's go into the lounge and sit by the fire, can you walk?"

Once she was seated comfortably, he wrapped a soft throw around her shoulders and poured two glasses of his special single malt. He downed his in one shot and handed the other to Rose, she wrinkled her nose.

"Can I have a chamomile tea instead?"

Minutes later he was back at her side with a glass of water glad to see she'd regained a little colour in her pallid cheeks, it was at this point that he also noticed the strange garment she had over her clothes. He'd never seen it before, in fact, he'd never seen anything like it before. Where had she got it from? His mind now took him to a place he wasn't familiar with, and it made him uncomfortable. Suspicion. Was the strange garment a piece of kinky lingerie gifted from a secret lover? The unpleasant sensation now burned the inside of his stomach causing him to feel sick. Surely, not his wife. Not Rose, she wouldn't be unfaithful to him, would she? She'd always stood unwaveringly at his side. Shaking his head, he tried to dislodge the noxious thought, and pasted on a weak smile.

"Sorry, the powers off, I can't boil the kettle."

Sighing, she knew she would have to offer an explanation of some sort, but where to begin? She didn't think he'd be open to the possibility of her being a witch, so she stuck to plan A.

"Another layer of dust had settled in the study, and I was just trying to get rid of it before it spread about the rest of the cottage."

She thought that her excuse sounded plausible enough, but Alan wasn't convinced.

Picking up the second glass of single malt he took a gulp, "So why did you open the window Rose in the middle of a storm?"

"I opened the window to shake the duster outside, but it coincided with the lightning strike, I think it might have hit the cottage." Pausing, she sipped her water while they both sat in the darkened room with the glow from the wood burner bathing them in a warm, soft light. "Is there any damage?"

The whiskey had now found its way into Alan's bloodstream and his body sagged, "I don't think so, I had a quick look outside before I came in. Are you feeling better now?"

Nodding, Rose put her glass down, I'm tired and I have a headache, but I'm okay."

Once more, he took her arm and helped her up, "Come on, time for bed."

Two glasses of single malt had Alan snoring in no time at all, while Rose on the other hand was wide awake. Her mind and body were buzzing as though she had been recharged with a surge of special energy. Excited, she knew she couldn't stay in bed, no, she had important things to do tonight. Glancing back at her sleeping husband, she slipped her feet into her comfy mules and wrapped her fleece dressing gown snugly around her body. Her first task was to hide her kimono, thankfully Alan hadn't noticed it. When she reached the kitchen she paused, the electricity was still off, but the full moon was bathing the room with a cold, silvery glow. Using her phone as a torch, she opened her herb and spice cupboard where she hid her secret potion, the one that Freya had made for her. Shaking the small bottle, she noticed it was nearly empty, would Freya make her some more? Longingly her eyes strayed to the kettle, but she knew there was no chance of a hot chocolate or chamomile tea yet, cold water would once more have to suffice. With the potent liquid now coursing through her veins she returned to the study and re lit her candles then made herself comfortable. Suddenly, a deep, bone aching shiver ran through her body, it was cold – icy cold, chilling her to the core.

Weak sunlight streamed in through the small windows of the wooden cabin where Alice sat at the kitchen table, which was now cloaked in a sombre black cloth. She was inconsolable. Sobs wracked her thin, pale body causing it to shake violently. Her lifelong friend Grace was sat at her side with an expression as desolate as the landscape beyond the cosy interior of the small home. The one, which just a few days ago had rung to the sound of friendly banter as the family had enjoyed each other's love. "Please try to eat something, I've made some food."

Forlorn, Alice mournfully shook her head, and stared across the room with unseeing eyes, how could she possibly eat now that her firstborn had perished? The pain she felt was unlike anything she'd previously experienced. She felt numb, drained of life. She knew that she'd never feel whole again. A part of her had died along with John.

Her husband ran his hand through his hair and turned to face the fire that Albert had built and replenished for the last few days. He couldn't bear to look at his wife knowing there was nothing at all he could do to lessen her crushing pain.

Albert was distraught too; he'd known the boy since he was a new-born, proudly laid in his mother's loving embrace. Yes, his friends needed them now more than ever before. "Grace is right, you've got to eat, both of you. You've still got David to think about, he's going to be lost without his big brother."

Jack realised Albert, his lifelong friend was only trying to be helpful, but he was beyond help. He'd never felt so bereft in his life. Even during the war when he lost comrades from his squadron, yes, he'd mourned and missed them, but this was something else entirely. Every breath he took was a mammoth effort. His lungs felt as though they too were full of the same glacial water that had taken his precious son away from him. How would they get through this?

"Where is David?" Panicked, Alices bloodshot eyes opened a little wider in alarm, looking for her youngest son.

Trying once more to comfort her friend, Grace stood and placed a hand on her shoulder, "He's next door with Scott."

Alice's shoulders slumped and she rested her aching head in her hands while Grace began to feel guilty, both of her beautiful children, were safe and well. She could only imagine the agony of losing a child. But what could she do to help? Her thoughts and actions seemed woefully inadequate. Survivor's guilt. She knew her kind-hearted son, Scott, would do his upmost to support David. They'd been best friends since they were toddlers together at their mother's knees.

A gentle knock on the cabin door gave Grace something to do. Helen, a local woman draped in a black shawl handed over a tray of freshly prepared sandwiches and fruit scones. "I've brought these for after the service."

Glad of the distraction, Grace accepted the welcome gift from her outstretched arms and invited her inside. Helens eyes were immediately drawn to the back of the room where a sombre sight caused a sharp intake of breath. It was the coffin. John's coffin. Made from polished Canadian maple. On top of it was a framed photo of the young man alongside two matching candlesticks holding slim, white candles, now flickering on the draught that had followed Helen into the room. Bowing her head Helen made the sign of the cross on her chest before turning away to meet a pitiful nod from Grace.

"Thank you, that's very kind." Silence returned hanging like a thick fog in the room. Grace longing for something to do with her hands walked over to the kettle. "Would you like a drink?"

Shaking her head Helen retreated towards the door eager to leave, the grief was palpable, "No, thank you, I'll see you in the chapel."

Alberts puffy eyes landed on the door after it had softly closed behind Helen, "I'll go and fetch David, it will soon be time to leave." Grateful of the reprieve, he inhaled the cold, crisp air hanging between the two houses wishing the dreadful day was over.

Several local men dressed in black with shovels over their shoulders nodded as they cleared a path through the deep snow, one of them stepped forward and spoke, it was Harry, "We're here to help carry the lad to chapel."

Albert hadn't doubted them for a minute, he knew the locals would stand by, as they always had in times of need. Soon, more families arrived with the women carrying bottles and trays of food for the wake. They'd do him proud.

A bright flash caused Rose's head to spin, where was she? Clutching at the bricks of the fireplace to steady herself before pulling herself upright, she swayed a little while trying to make sense of her surroundings. She was in the study. Breathing heavy, as though she'd been for a brisk walk, she looked about her somewhat bewildered. Yes, she was in the study and the lights had come back on. The sound of Edward striking the hour grounded her a little, it was midnight.

Now able to make a cup of calming chamomile tea Rose took it back to bed and sat up beside her husband who was still sleeping soundly. Her mind strayed back to the vision, and she quietly relived every second in her mind, committing minute details to her memory bank. She'd write it down in her dream diary in the morning.

"The candlesticks! The candlesticks were on top of the coffin!"

Her excitement had made her forget where she was, and Alan opened his eyes signalling a slight alarm.

"What... where... Rose... are you okay?"

He was now sat bolt upright causing Rose to spill her tea, sighing, she jumped out of bed to reach for the box of tissues.

"Yes, I'm good, just couldn't sleep. I didn't mean to disturb you. Sorry."

Groggily, Alan rubbed his eyes and settled back down pulling the duvet off Rose as he turned over. But she didn't mind, she was still too excited to sleep so once more padded down the corridor to the spare room where she hid her dream diary under the mattress. Alan would never think to look there. A depressing thought momentarily flittered across her mind, should they just have separate bedrooms now?

17.

Trying to go about her everyday chores was a distraction for Rose, but her mind wandered frequently to the candlesticks. Her candlesticks. She felt sure they were the very same ones that had been placed on top of John's coffin. Frustrated, she left her laundry behind and idly picked them up for the umpteenth time. But how could she be sure? Stroking their polished surface her fingers lazily traced the patterns in the wood, the spalted areas that made them so distinctive. Underneath she re-read the one identifying word. Ontario. They were from Canada. She'd trawled the internet for clues and found that the Royal Canadian Air Force were indeed allies in the second world war, flying alongside the RAF. And she knew that Jack, John's father had flown a spitfire in the war. Closing her eyes once more she recalled the image of John's coffin and in her heart, she knew that they were the same pair of candlesticks. But how did they end up here in England? And what did it have to do with her? She needed to share her experience with Freya. She might have some ideas.

Confused and frustrated she called her friend who arrived within the hour. Freya listened carefully without interruption while Rose described every minute detail of the previous night's events. Freya was fascinated and took the candlesticks from Rose holding them tight to her chest.

"Can I go into the spare room and sit on the rocking chair?"

"Sure, if you think it will help."

Once in the spare room Freya made herself comfortable and soon her eyes were closed, and her features contorted as though she might be in pain. Stepping towards her Rose held out her hand then stopped herself, Freya was clearly channelling all of her energy in search of answers. But would she succeed?

Several minutes passed before she opened her eyes again and she looked exhausted, "Well?" Rose questioned optimistically.

"I'm not sure."

"But ... but you felt something?"

"Well, yes. I think so." Wide eyed, Rose stood still waiting for Freya to recover fully. "I know this sounds strange, but I felt like I was on a boat."

Levering herself out of the old chair Freya wobbled and placed a hand on the window sill to steady herself. Instinctively, Rose reached out and grasped her hand, "Let's go into the lounge, I'll get you a cup of tea.

Back at her side with refreshments Rose continued with her investigations, "So, what sort of boat was it, big or small?"

"Oh, big, more of a ship than a boat, a ferry perhaps or even a cruise liner – not that I've ever been on one."

"But, how do you know?"

"It was moving, pitching and rolling a little and I could hear the waves lapping on the sides of the vessel, a bit like in the movies."

One of the holidays that Rose, and Alan had taken with their teenage daughters suddenly came tumbling back from her memory, a cruise which included a lengthy spell sailing between Madeira and Morocco. The sea had been so rough, and the slightly anxious family had spent a sleepless night being tossed about in their bunks feeling rather queasy. Shaking her head, she tried to concentrate on Freya's revelation.

"Erm, did you, erm, see anyone or anything?"

Freya dunked a digestive biscuit in her cup and somehow managed to get the soggy end into her mouth before it disintegrated, she then wiped her lips on her sleeve.

"No, sorry, it was just a feeling. A sensation as though I was on a ship crossing a large body of water. Oh, and it was cold." Placing her cup back on the tray she shrugged, "Not much help, is it? You're better at this than me." Suddenly Freya's head snapped up as though she'd thought of something exciting, "Do you have any loose leaf tea?"

Frowning, Rose considered the question, "You mean tea leaves, the old-fashioned stuff?" Freya nodded hopefully. "No, sorry, I always use tea bags." Rose sat down then suddenly jumped back up, "But I have got dried herbs, chamomile, sage, rosemary and a few others that I grew last year. I could make a chamomile tea, would that work?"

"Only one way to find out!"

In the kitchen Rose handed her friend a delicate, pale blue China cup and saucer that had belonged to her mother, but Freya quickly held up her hand, "No, you have to make it for yourself, but you must follow my instructions carefully."

Squaring her shoulders Rose took a deep breath and filled the kettle, then looked back at her mentor.

"First, you need to clear your mind and think about the question you want answering."

"Oh!" Rose's eyes found Freya's, "But I've got lots of questions."

"Be patient Rose, only one at a time. Are you ready?"

"Erm, can I have a minute to think?"

"Sure, you only get one chance at this today."

Inhaling deeply Rose pondered her many unsolved mysteries, which was most important? She wasn't sure. Then an image of John's coffin slid its way into her thoughts. Yes. It had to be the candlesticks. How on earth had they found their way into her possession when they originated form the other side of the globe in Canada? Signalling she was now ready Rose nodded, then scooped up the candlesticks and placed them on the breakfast bar. "Let's do this."

"Right, take a pinch of the tea and sprinkle it into the cup then pour over the boiling water."

Following the instructions Rose concentrated on the candlesticks while she inhaled the aroma of the fruity brew.

"Good, now place the saucer on top and leave it to steep for a minute."

Again, Rose did as she was asked while trying to keep the image of poor John's funeral in her mind.

"Okay, now you need to concentrate and quietly reflect on the mystery you have chosen."

Rose was about to speak but again Freya held up her hand, "Don't tell me anything." Following a lengthy pause Freya continued, "Good, now remove the saucer and pick the cup up with your left hand and drink it when you're ready."

Slowly, Rose carried the precious liquid and placed it on the breakfast bar next to the candlesticks and sat down, Freya joined her, and the friends sat in silence. Rose concentrated while sipping her magic brew. Once most of it was consumed Freya spoke again.

"Fab, now with the cup still in your left-hand, swirl the remains anticlockwise three times."

Rose did this then looked back up into Freya's eyes.

"Good, now for the tricky bit – quickly turn it upside down onto the saucer trying not to spill any." Anxiously, Rose's eyes widened.

"Go on, you can do it."

With a slight tremble Rose swiftly upended the small teacup and placed it onto the blue China saucer with its contents intact. Her shoulders slumped as the tension left her body thankful that she'd successfully fulfilled her part of the ritual.

Another lengthy pause followed before Freya reached over and slid the cup and saucer towards her, closed her eyes and took several deep breaths, then with her right hand she took hold of the delicate handle and turned the teacup over before gazing into its depths. Rose knew not to interrupt her friend as she silently transcended into the zone.

Fidgeting with her wedding ring she waited anxiously

for her friend to speak, but Freya remained silent still gazing into the cup, then she closed her eyes again while Rose impatiently observed the varied expressions that fleetingly rearranged her familiar features. Freya took another deep breath, opened her sparkling green eyes and sat back.

"Well, what did you see?"

Smiling, Freya deliberated her response carefully, she knew that Rose would hang onto her every word. Her sitters always did, but this was no ordinary sitter – it was Rose, her best friend. She'd have to tread lightly.

"Well, tasseography is as much an art as it is a science." Rose's brow furrowed but she remained silent. "It's about interpretation. My gut feelings and instincts of the shapes that have presented themselves and their distribution. Do you understand?"

Nodding in compliance, she urged Freya to continue.

"Okay, so the first thing that jumped out at me was the shape of a ship or a boat way down in the bottom of the cup, can you see it?" Squinting, Rose leaned over. "There, over to the right-hand side."

Tilting the cup over Rose peered into the bottom of the vessel, "Oh yes, I think I can see that now, it does look a bit like a boat doesn't it?"

"It does, and because it's way down on the base of the

cup it means it's in the past." Trying to digest the words Rose held her breath. "And it's on the right-hand side of the cup so that indicates success."

"So, am I going on a cruise?"

Disappointed, Freya leaned back wondering how she could manage her friend's expectations. "No Rose, it's in the past. It's not always about predicting the future, that's a myth."

"Oh, we have been on a few cruises."

Freya was trying to gently steer Rose to be a bit more open minded, but she needed to be patient "Remember, it's not really about you, it's about the candlesticks isn't it?" Feeling a bit foolish Rose flushed and Freya continued. "So, my interpretation is about them – they came over on a boat, a long time ago and it was a positive outcome. That also ties in with the sensations I had when I held them. Yes?" Nodding again Rose kept quiet wanting to hear more. "Further up, about two thirds of the way right by the handle is the shape of a hammer."

"Ooh, yes, I can see that. But what does a hammer mean?"

"I think it represents a challenge. It's on the midline between left and right."

"Oh, is that bad?"

"If it were on its own, I might think that, but look a little closer. Can you see a tiny fish just to the right of it, slightly higher up?"

"Oh yes, I can see that now that you've pointed it out."

"Well, that indicates that the challenge is tied to the fish."

Rose's head snapped up. "What does a fish mean?"

"A fish could mean good news from another country, and because it's a little higher up, nearer the rim it's in the future. Are you following me?"

"Yes, I think so." Rose screwed her eyes tight shut and shook her shoulders out. "So, the hammer – the challenge is that in the future too?"

"That appears to me to be in the present, which would tie in – you are facing a challenge right now to decipher the meanings of your visions. Yes?" Pondering this information Rose nodded and stopped herself from blurting out that her marriage was also a bit challenging at the moment too. But this wasn't about her, was it?

"Okay, so the fish, it's higher up, nearer the rim, so what does that mean?"

"Ah, that's in the future."

The two friends smiled at each other, and Rose sat back. "So, I'm currently experiencing a challenge, but some good news is coming from another country. Is that it?"

"Not everything, there's the favourable boat journey from the past and if you look more carefully there's a pattern near the bottom of the cup, again on the midline between left and right can you see it?"

"Yes, but it's miniscule."

"It is, but look harder, can you make out a letter?"

"Ooh!" Rose leaned over once more. "I need my reading glasses, don't move." On her return she concentrated on the small pattern, it was comprised of five or six small specs of chamomile. "Sorry, you're going to have to help me out."

"Well, I can see a capital W."

Excitedly, Rose looked again, "Yes! Yes! I can see it now!"

"Good. It's way in the past too. Does it mean anything significant to you?"

A frown of concentration furrowed Rose's brow as she thought of her parents then grandparents, none of their names had begun with W. She'd had an old school friend called Wendy, but they hadn't kept in touch, so it probably wasn't her either. "No, I can't think of anyone from my past beginning with W that would be significant."

"There you go, that's another challenge for you. Figuring out who or what W is."

Deep in thought Rose sat back on her stool still running through possible candidates beginning with W. Standing and reaching for her bag Freya put her hand on Rose's shoulder.

"I'm going now. Good luck. You will succeed Rose."

18.

The rest of the week was a blur for Rose as she spent every waking minute thinking about her mystery, and most nights dreaming about it too. Just who was this elusive person beginning with W? She had no idea. The more she thought about it, the more baffled she became.

On Saturday morning, the doorbell rang at eight-thirty. Alan opened the door to find Charlie with his toolbox in one hand and a length of wood in the other.

"Morning. Thought I'd make a start on the fireplace today, if that's okay."

Sighing, Alan paused and pressed his lips into a hard, thin line before speaking. "Are you sure that you know what you're taking on?"

Undeterred by the negative comment, Charlie stepped inside. "Yes sir, and you'll hardly know I'm here. Promise I won't make a mess."

Turning, Alan shrugged his shoulders and shouted down the hallway. "It's for you Rose. I'm going in the garage."

Eager for Charlie to make a start on the project, Rose carried all of Alan's precious trophies into the spare room and spread dust sheets over the carpet. Better to be safe than sorry she mused. A short while later, hearing the sound of banging, she popped her head round the study door to check on progress. Charlie was prising away the damaged piece of wood that framed the brick work around the hearth.

"How's it going Charlie?"

"Oh, I'm just removing this frame so I can repair the damage. It will be as good as new when it's finished, you'll hardly see the join."

Rose was unconvinced, but decided not to voice her negative thoughts. "Erm, what about those bricks? They're loose. Some of the old mortar has crumbled away."

"Don't worry, I'm going to put them back and re-point, then I'll repair the old frame."

"But the frame is carved and it's a different colour from the new wood that you've brought."

"Trust me, it will all be matched up again and stained the same colour."

Signalling the end of the conversation, Charlie picked up the new wood and reached for his tape measure. Rose took the hint and decided to try and keep out of his way. She couldn't possibly bake again; the freezer was already bursting with scones and pasties. Looking out of the window, she noticed that the sun was breaking through the clouds and decided to go and do some gardening instead. Spring was here at last. In fact, it would be the spring equinox shortly. She'd love to celebrate it with Freya, she thought, as her mind wandered back to the twenty-first of December. Perhaps they could do it at her house this time. Mm, but what about Alan? That could be a problem.

Once outside with her secateurs Rose began snipping away, lost in thought, when she heard a voice. Stopping, she listened again then saw Charlie striding towards her. His face was flushed and his eyes wide.

"Excuse me!"

"Hi Charlie, is there a problem?"

"Oh no, not a problem, but I've found this."

"What is it?"

"A small wooden box. It's covered in dust and cobwebs."

Excited, Rose took it from his outstretched hands. "Where was it?"

"Hidden behind one of the loose bricks. Have you got a soft brush? I'll clean it up for you."

Rose quickly found him a paint brush and eagerly watched while Charlie set to work.

Suddenly he looked up and beamed. "Wow! It's

engraved"

"What does it say? Let me see!"

Astonished, Rose ran her fingers over the small, engraved box. "William and Anne." Rose's face lit up. "And there's a date. 1860."

Striding over to the patio table, she placed it down. "What's inside?"

"May I?"

Nodding, Rose slid the precious box across the table to Charlie. Carefully, he wiggled the lid; it was a tight fit but at last it came off in his hand. The box was lined with yellowed linen and a small object, wrapped in more linen, nestled in the bottom. With trembling hands, Rose picked it up and slowly unwrapped the treasure to reveal a plain gold band. It was tiny. Hesitating, she tried it for size, but it would only fit on her little finger. Inside the ring was a hallmark, too small to read with the naked eye.

"It looks like a gold wedding ring."

Charlie nodded and picked the box up, carefully turning it over to reveal more letters and a date. B. M. 1862. But these letters were different, just scratched into the surface of the wood, not carved with great care like the letters on the lid.

"B. M." Astonished, Rose looked up. "Who were William

and Anne? And who is B. M?"

"I have no idea. Isn't it exciting?"

"It's a puzzle, that's for sure." Suddenly Rose remembered the letter W from her tea leaf reading. Was this the significant W? But she decided not to share that snippet of information with Charlie; she didn't want to scare him away. Anyway, wasn't that W supposed to be connected to the candlesticks? Now she was even more confused.

"Well, I'd better get back to work. I'll let you know if I find anything else."

Bursting with excitement, she took several photos of the box and ring then sent them to Freya, who replied instantly.

Wow! That's amazing, another piece of the jigsaw puzzle. I'm looking forward to handling them. Bring them over when you're free.

Itching to visit her friend, Rose consulted her diary. She couldn't go this weekend and leave Charlie; Alan wouldn't be at all impressed. No, it would have to be one day next week. Before long she was interrupted by Charlie again.

"Sorry to disturb you again but I've found an old shoe."

"Oh, how bizarre. Where is it?"

"Follow me. It's fixed into the mortar."

Once in the study, Charlie knelt down and shone his torch up inside the chimney void. Rose followed suit and enthusiastically peered into the darkness. "I can't see anything."

"Just there, on the left, about six brick courses up. Can you see it?" Adjusting her position Rose crouched and banged her head. "Oh dear, are you okay?"

Sagging with deflation, Rose sat on her haunches and rubbed her forehead where she could feel a small lump emerging. Irritated she snapped, "Yes, it's nothing, but I can't see this elusive shoe!"

Charlie helped her onto a chair and fussed for a while then had an idea. With the torch wedged in position, he twisted his lithe body and inserted a long arm into the space to take a photo. Sooty but triumphant, he showed the image to Rose.

"Oh yes! I can see it now. How strange. Why on earth is there an old shoe up the chimney?"

Crouching at her side he shrugged, "Well, it's actually not that unusual. In the olden days, shoes were often concealed in properties for protection."

"Really? Have you come across this before?"

Charlie scratched his chin while he thought back to the few old buildings he'd worked on previously. "Yes, just once, we found a child's shoe hidden above a door lintel. Apparently they're meant to ward off danger and evil spirits."

"Well, I suppose we'd better leave it where it is then."

Nodding, Charlie agreed. "I'll send you the photo."

With the small box of treasure clutched tightly in her grip, Rose left Charlie to continue his task while she went out to the garage to tell Alan.

But Alan didn't even bother to look up from his greasy engine. "Thanks, Love, just put it on the bench."

Tutting, Rose bristled, "It's not coffee Alan, it's treasure!" Now by his side she held the small box out in front of him. Perplexed, he reached out to take it from her, but she quickly pulled it back. "Don't touch it with your filthy hands! Come inside and get cleaned up first."

Trying to hide his irritation at the disruption, Alan wiped his oily hands on a rag and followed his wife into the kitchen, keeping his emotions to himself as he always did. With the small box now safely on the pine table, Rose removed the lid and passed it to him. "Look, it's engraved."

Alan read the inscription out loud, "William and Anne. 1860. Intriguing. What's inside?"

Carefully unwrapping the delicate wedding ring, she handed it to Alan. "It's a wedding ring."

"Yes, that much is obvious, and it's hallmarked, but it's too tiny to read. The big question is – who did it belong to?"

Handing the ring back to Rose, he picked the box up and shrugged. "Well, I'm no detective but I'd say it belonged to Anne. Perhaps William and Anne were married in 1860."

Rose's shoulders sagged. "Yes, but why is it in this box in *our* cottage? And what happened to them?"

Alan, now sensing his wife's frustration, turned to fill up the kettle. "Let's have a coffee while we think about it." As an afterthought he added, "Does that young lad want some?"

"Well, why don't you ask him? And he has a name. Charlie."

Charlie declined coffee but accepted a glass of fruit juice accompanied by a chocolate muffin. Once his glass was drained, he wiped the back of his hand across his mouth and grinned. "Have you found out who William and Anne were yet?"

Rose looked back at the young man. "Sadly not."

"It shouldn't be too difficult, you've got names, dates and presumably this address. There must be village records somewhere."

"Of course! Why didn't I think of that? I'll log back onto

the ancestry website again."

With both men eager to get back to their tasks, Rose finished her coffee and turned her laptop on.

19.

Meticulously, Rose revisited the archives of the local parish council, which consisted of twenty-two pages of incredibly difficult to read, ink-smudged, cursive writing. Frustratingly, many of the old properties were numbered incorrectly or, like her cottage, had previously had their names changed, which slowed down her progress somewhat. An old map of the village that Alan had previously found online and had framed, which dated from 1854, helped as she was able to use the pub as a reference point. It was later that afternoon when Rose had her 'Eureka moment'.

"Oh, my goodness!" She shouted, into the empty room.

Charlie had finished for the day and Alan was still restoring some precious item in his man cave. Exhausted but thrilled, she rolled her aching shoulders, removed her glasses, and leaned back in her chair. She'd found William and Anne on the 1861 census living in *her* cottage. William Mackley was a carpenter aged thirty-four and had been born in Ireland. His wife Anne, who had been born in the parish, was twenty-two and her maiden name had been Stocks. Rose struggled to read the spidery handwriting that was entered under the column for Anne's occupation. Perhaps Alan could make it out?

Thrilled, she rushed out to her husband. "I've found

them! Alan, I've found them!"

"Well done. I'll be in shortly then you can show me."

After supper, Rose showed Alan the website. "I've been looking for months for B. M. with no luck but now I've found him; he's called William Mackley."

A frown crossed Alan's brow. "How can you have been looking for months when you only found the box today?"

Realising her mistake, Rose flushed. "Erm…"

"Erm, what?"

"Well, do you remember the old rocking chair?"

Alan nodded, "The one that we threw out?"

"I didn't throw it out, Alan, it's in the spare room." This time Alan remained silent and waited for Rose to continue. "I like it and it's staying."

"Okay."

"Well, it's got B. M. 1854 engraved underneath the seat. I've spent ages on an ancestry website looking for B. M. in 1854."

"Wow! And now you've found him. So, we have to presume that William preferred to be called Bill or Billy, hence the B.M."

"Yes, that's why I couldn't find him. And he's a carpenter, so that'll be why he's got a ..." Rose quickly stopped herself from finishing the sentence *'finger missing'*. "Erm, that's erm, why his initials are under the chair. He must have made it!"

"Almost certainly." Alan was still busy scrolling through the ancestry website and thankfully seemed too engrossed to have noticed Rose's slip up. "It's an incredible site. Will you be able to find anything about Anne?"

"Oh, yes. I was going to ask you, what do you think this word here says about her occupation?"

Squinting, Alan pulled the laptop closer. "Mm, I'm not sure, I think it begins with M and that letter looks like F. But it would have been very unusual for a married woman to have had a job back then. They would all have been housewives and mothers."

Rose looked at her husband and thought that he would have suited life in the 1800's with a subservient wife running around after him. Frustrated, she took the mouse from Alan and sat in front of her laptop for another half-an-hour before Edward stuck ten. "Bedtime, I think."

Rose waited patiently for Alan to fall into a deep sleep then climbed out of bed as stealthily as possible. In the kitchen she made herself a cup of mugwort tea in the blue China teacup which had previously belonged to her mother and picked up the small wooden box. With the box in her right hand and the cup in her left she padded into the spare room and made herself comfortable on the old rocking chair, the one that William Mackley had made in 1854.

Once she felt settled, she took the ring out of its box where it had lain hidden for over one hundred and sixty years and gently slid it down the little finger on her right hand. It was a snug fit, but she could just manage to twist it around in a clockwise direction three times. She wasn't sure why she had done that, but it seemed like something Freya would have done. It felt right. With the wooden box still on her lap, she calmly sipped her tea while concentrating on the things that she already knew about William and Anne.

William Mackley had arrived from Ireland some time before 1854 and he was thirty-four years old in 1861. His wife, Anne, was twenty-two and they'd married in the parish a year earlier. He was a carpenter, but Rose couldn't decipher what Anne did for a job. Placing the empty cup on the window sill, Rose took three deep breaths and leaned back into the soft cushions trying desperately to conjure up his image. But nothing came. Frustrated, she opened her eyes and stared around the darkened room. It didn't feel right. Something was missing. Beginning to feel annoyed with herself, she stood up and wandered out into the hall. It felt empty too.

Looking around, she found herself being drawn to the study door. What was it about the study? It was hardly ever used. Cautiously, she entered and her eyes were immediately drawn to the fireplace. An ambient glow filtered in through the window as the midsummer sun showed her reluctance to retire and Rose knelt on the floor. The piece of damaged wood lay discarded by her side. Reaching out, she picked it up and held it close while her fingers traced the delicately carved pattern of what appeared to be leaves. Where the design finished, her fingers continued onto what had now become familiar to Rose. B. M. It was like braille to her. William had clearly left his mark here as well. Fascinated, Rose held it to her bosom. William had made this fireplace. What else had he made in the cottage?

Closing her eyes once more Rose continued to run her fingers over the initials; it felt comforting as though it were soothing her frustrations. Soon, she felt a cold chill climb each individual vertebrae of her spine as though it were a ladder and before long, it entered her skull.

Suddenly, she found herself observing helplessly as a wiry haired, old man tried his best to revive poor Anne. She was in this very room with them, their study, but back then it was clearly a cosy bedroom with a rocking chair by the fire. Her rocking chair. She watched events unfold in front of her. Before her, a fire burned brightly in the grate while William cradled his wife's limp head in his arms. At the same time, he whispered to the rosary beads laid across her chest. A puddle of shocking red blood had pooled on the bed between her legs, Rose could smell its metallic tang, a stark contrast with the pure white sheets and the deathly pallor of her skin.

The wiry haired man stepped back and bowed his head. "She's gone. I'm sorry."

"But surely there's something you can do Dr James!" the older woman shouted, wringing her hands.

Shaking his head he sighed, avoiding eye contact with Ethel, the older woman, whom he'd known most of his life. She was now distraught. Anne was, after all her own dear daughter. Despite being an experienced midwife, there was nothing more Ethel could do for the girl now.

Again, William let out a low animalistic moan, making the doctor wince and step back. "You need to focus on the infant; she'll need a nurse."

Ethel knew they were well meant words, but they cut deep into her core. Her first grandchild, a precious girl, who she couldn't even feed, but she'd need to keep her close so she could nurture the gift that was often passed down from mother to eldest daughter in this family. It had been so for countless generations. Anne had possessed the gift herself and now she'd sacrificed her own life to bring the next wise woman into the family. Yes, it was her responsibility now to ensure it lived on in this new life. But the doctor was right, the baby needed a nurse, and quickly.

Dr James walked over to Anne's limp body and pulled a sheet over her. "Perhaps you should go and visit Lydia Butterwick, down at the farm. She had a stillbirth a couple of weeks ago."

Ethel remembered it well, a little boy, premature and lifeless. She recalled praying that her daughter wouldn't suffer the same fate – but this was even worse, much worse. The baby would have to stay with Lydia – if she'd have her. But, in her heart, she knew that she would. Everyone helped each other in the village. It would only be for a few months anyway; they'd wean her early onto goat's milk. It had been done before. Then she could take care of her, teach her all she'd need to know to keep the line going, and one day she'd pass it on to her daughter. Yes. Despite her overbearing grief Ethel knew that all was not lost.

The sound of running water brought Rose back to the present; bleary eyed she looked around. She was in the study. Footsteps in the hall alerted her that Alan was up. Hopefully, he'd assume she'd gone into the spare room. Edward chimed four am. Dawn. Wrapping her bathrobe over the secret kimono, she stood on wobbly legs fighting the pain of pins and needles as the blood flow returned to her dead feet. Hobbling into the kitchen, she got a glass of water then went back to their room where her husband was back in bed.

"Sorry, I didn't mean to disturb you; I'd got a nasty cramp and needed a drink."

"I woke up and you'd gone again so I assumed you were bed hopping."

Rose lay beside her husband, expecting him to start snoring, but for once he was quiet. Alan wasn't asleep. He was concerned about his wife. Why was she acting bizarrely? What was that strange garment that she wore in secret? Was she having late night phone calls with another man? Then another disturbing thought entered his mind. Was it a woman? Was it Freya leading her astray? After all, she had spent a night with her! Alan continued to lay silently at Rose's side with the unpleasant taste of regret in his mouth.

20.

The following morning was Sunday. Alan woke early and took Rose a cup of tea, wondering if he should broach the subject of her strange behaviour.

Smiling, he offered her a peck on the cheek. "Good morning, is your leg better?"

Frowning, Rose tried to remember last night's events, taking time to rearrange her pillows while she gathered her thoughts.

"Yes, just cramp. It was nothing serious."

Sipping his tea in silence, Alan wondered where to begin. "Erm, I was thinking, perhaps we need a holiday."

Shocked by his comment, Rose put her tea down and stared at him. "A holiday. But you never want to go on holiday! Are you okay?"

An uneasy silence followed where Rose thought back to the numerous times before online bookings existed that she'd visited the local travel agents and returned with a pile of holiday brochures to wade through. She could never get him interested. She'd even gone away with the girls during their university holidays without him. As long as there were plenty of ready meals in the freezer, he was happy.

Choosing his words carefully, he broke the silence. "Well, I was actually wondering if you were okay – you've been acting, erm, a bit out of character recently."

As if on cue, Rose could feel a hot flush, beginning at her core, that radiated up her chest and neck before reaching her head. She felt like she might explode, and she was getting a headache too. Stress always exacerbated her symptoms.

Stretching for her glass of water, she stuttered, "H… have I? Well, it wasn't intentional."

Alan didn't speak; he leant over and took her hand.

Deflating a little she continued, "Don't worry. It's just the menopause Alan – it seems to be getting worse."

"Mm, well I think you should go back to see the doctor; those pills clearly aren't working."

Rose flung the duvet off herself, signalling the end of their conversation. "I'll ring them tomorrow. I'm going for a cool shower."

After breakfast they went for a walk through the village with Nellie. Alan tried to bring up the subject of a holiday again, but Rose managed to change the subject, commenting on the pretty wildflowers down the lane and how fast the lambs were growing. When they returned, Alan didn't go into his garage but sat on his iPad for the morning while Rose fussed about in the kitchen.

Busy preparing vegetables for Sunday lunch, she jumped when he approached her from behind and placed a hand on her shoulder. "I've made a short list of five holidays that are available next month that fit in with my motor sport calendar and work commitments."

Irritated, Rose wiped her hands on her apron. Why was it always about what worked for him? She turned around and sighed then followed him to the breakfast bar where he showed her his choices. A chalet in the Italian Alps was at the top of his list followed by a villa in the Spanish Pyrenees.

"Why the mountains? A cruise would be more relaxing."

"There are some fantastic roads and mountain passes — and you'd enjoy the scenery. Cruises are a bit — well — boring."

Rose held up her hand. "No Alan! I'm not going on a driving holiday. Anyway, what would we do with Nellie?"

"Somebody would have her, or she could go into boarding kennels..."

Alan didn't get chance to finish his sentence.

"Not happening!"

Lunch was eaten in stony silence and Alan was relieved to go back to work on Monday morning. What was wrong with his wife?

Rose too was glad to have some space and went and sat in the study where she recalled Saturday night's vision. Poor Anne had died during childbirth; her mother, Ethel was a midwife and wise woman. What exactly did that mean? Rose thought back to the illegible writing entered under Anne's occupation. Midwife. Yes, that's what it said. She too had been a midwife. How ironic that she would have helped numerous other women through childbirth yet hadn't survived the ordeal herself. There would have been no pain relief or caesarean sections and clearly no blood transfusions. Poor Anne. And what happened to the baby? Her daughter. Did she survive?

Rose couldn't decide what to do next. She was itching to ring Freya to tell her all about her experience, but she was also desperate to find out more. What year had Anne passed away? What was the baby called? Did Ethel take care of her? Did William remarry? It seemed the more she learned, the more questions she had.

The rest of the morning flew by in a blur as Rose sat glued to her laptop, seeking answers to her questions. According to a dictionary, a wise woman was *'a woman considered to be knowledgeable in matters such as herbal healing, magic charms or other traditional lore.'*

Wow! In other words – a witch! Anne and her mother had both been witches. That's what Ethel meant by 'the gift'. Did the baby inherit the gift too?

Rose continued talking to herself while she did her research, but was soon interrupted by the doorbell. She wasn't expecting anyone. Frustrated by the intrusion, she opened the door to find Freya with a bottle in her outstretched hand.

"Good afternoon, hope you're not too busy. I've made so much elderflower cordial over the weekend, I thought you might like some."

Hugging her friend, Rose seemed surprised. "Is it afternoon already? I must have lost track of time. I've got so much to tell you! Have you eaten?"

Once in the kitchen, the two friends shared a goat's cheese salad while Rose brought Freya up to speed with her latest discoveries.

"Wow! Rose, that's amazing! I'm speechless. And this little box is exquisite. William was clearly a very talented carpenter."

"I know." Rose sat back on her buffet while a frown wrinkled her features.

"What's wrong? I know it can take its toll."

"It's not me, it's Alan. I'm sure he thinks I'm losing the plot. He's even suggested that we go on holiday. I've always previously had to drag him away! I'm sure he suspects something."

While savouring a large wedge of homemade lemon drizzle cake, Freya considered the situation. "What do you want Rose?"

"I'm not sure anymore. I'm baffled. Why me? Why is this happening to me? And why now?"

Concerned that she might confuse her friend even more, Freya paused to form her response. "Because you have the gift too. We both do."

"You mean, I'm actually a real witch?"

"Yes. We both are."

"Then why has this never happened to me before?"

"Well, I suspect it's because you were always busy with your job and your family. You were distracted – not open minded enough." Rose took her time to absorb the words, but Freya continued her explanation. "It was fate. You were drawn to this village, this very cottage. And we were drawn together for some purpose. It was meant to be."

Struggling to get her head around the enormity of her friend's words, Rose sat in silence for a long while.

"So, I kind of get the connection with the cottage and William; it's almost as if he's stuck here. A ghost perhaps. But what about the other dreams and visions? What about Joseph and Ester? And poor John - drowning under the frozen lake – and- and - Sabine!" Rose's words started to break up as she began to sob and lose control of her emotions.

After comforting her friend, Freya tried to offer a plausible explanation. "Well, I'm no expert but I think the other visions were possibly a practice. I know that sounds weird. The antiques that you bought were clearly oozing their history and you were learning how to pick up on it. Does that make sense?"

Wide eyed, Rose nodded. "I suppose. But how do I find out what happened to them?"

"Well, you know that John died and that the candlesticks came from Ontario."

"Yes, they came on a boat, and it was cold…"

"Mm, I've been thinking about that. The boat trip could have been William coming over from Ireland."

"But you were holding the candlesticks when you felt that connection."

"Yes, I was, but I was also sitting in the rocking chair that William made – in this very cottage. I do think you're right though. I think he's still here."

Freya's comment spooked Rose. "Really? A ghost? Do you think this place is haunted?"

"Calm down." Again, Freya took Rose's hand and looked into her face. "Not in a threatening, scary sort of way. But perhaps he's trying to tell you something."

Rose's eyes were now like saucers. "Like what?"

"I don't know, but I don't think you have anything to fear." The two women looked at each other, trying to absorb their situation. "Perhaps Alan's right. You need to take a break – to get away and clear your head. Put things into perspective. There is so much energy in this cottage, it's clouding your thoughts."

"Possibly, but what should I tell Alan? And there's no way I'm going abroad just now. I'm not leaving Nellie in the kennels."

"You don't need to; she knows me. I'll come and stay with her. Why don't you suggest a long weekend away? A staycation. And you can tell Alan as much or as little as you like. But one thing's for sure, you can't keep it a secret from him forever."

21.

After Freya had left, Rose sat in the lounge and pondered. It was probably better to stay out of the study for the rest of the day to clear her head. The lounge was the safest place. Yes, she'd never felt anything mysterious in the lounge. The more she thought about it, the more it made perfect sense to her. The front half of the cottage had been added on in nineteen-twenty. William would have been about one hundred years old by then. Long dead. Only the kitchen and study existed during his lifetime. Rose had another thought and was about to look online to check the timeline she'd written to remind her who occupied her cottage then, but Freya's words came back to her. *"Perhaps Alan's right. You need to take a break – to get away and clear your head."*

By the time Alan returned from work, Rose had booked a long weekend away in Scotland.

"Loch Fyne! Wow!"

Concerned, Rose stared back at her husband's wide eyes, "Are you cross? Is it too far? I can cancel it if…"

"No, it's perfect. What a lovely surprise." Alan walked over and embraced his wife. "It will only take about four hours. What made you choose Loch Fyne?"

"It looked remote. Peaceful. A place to escape. And the

website mentions a superb driving road..."

"Yes, it's called 'Rest and be thankful' - that was very thoughtful of you."

Relations between Rose and Alan had improved slightly as they both made a special effort. When their holiday weekend drew closer, Rose was actually looking forward to it. Alan went to collect Freya early on their departure morning and waited patiently for Rose to stop fussing over Nellie and her daily routine, but at last they were ready to leave. Freya had been itching to spend some time alone in the cottage, she knew it was a special building. She'd felt it the first time she entered the cosy kitchen. It was a shame, she thought, that it hadn't coincided with the summer solstice, or even a full moon. No, she'd had to spend those recent events alone as Rose felt that it wasn't a good time to leave Alan. 'It would raise his suspicions', she'd said. But none the less, Freya was optimistic that something, or someone would reveal themselves to her now. Deep in her core, she knew there was a spiritual connection. If she was patient, this tangled web would eventually become clear.

After a long walk with Nellie, Freya returned to the cottage for a light lunch – a bowl of fresh fruit salad with a large glass of water. Today she needed to detox her system. Next, she set about her cleansing routine. The cottage was as usual, spotless. But the cleansing she had in mind wasn't to remove dust and dirt. No, it was to cleanse the space, remove any toxic vibes and unwanted auras. Her first task was to get the new besom that she'd made specially. It wasn't very big, a mini besom, small enough to fit in her case, but that didn't matter. It was the ritual that mattered. While symbolically sweeping each room, she chanted, making sure the doors and windows were wide open, giving bad entities an easy exit route. Nellie was fascinated, cocking her head quizzically to one side, probably wondering what was happening. Could she feel the spirits too? Freya thought that she probably could. Animals were very intuitive. Her next task was to sprinkle a little salt in front of the windows and doors so spirits with evil intentions couldn't enter. Once Freya was satisfied, she picked up the sage smudge stick that she'd made for this very occasion and, after wafting the smoke around herself and Nellie, she ceremoniously walked around every room, leaving no corner untouched, wafting the smoke with a pheasant's tail feather that she'd found on her walk. It had taken most of the afternoon, but at last she was satisfied. The cottage was prepared.

By teatime, Nellie was whinging to be fed and taken on another walk. Freya didn't mind, she'd grown fond of the little dog and enjoyed her company. After another bowl of fruit and a cup of fennel tea, Freya was about to prepare a bath when her phone rang. It was Rose.

"How's Nellie? Has she eaten? I do hope she's not pining for me. I've sent you several texts."

"Sorry, we've just been for a long walk, and I didn't take my phone. Stop worrying. Nellie's absolutely fine, and yes, she's eating. Anyway, how's the hotel? Are you having a good time?"

"Oh, good. Is she missing me?"

"Not as much as you're missing her! Try and relax Rose; stay in the present and enjoy some time with Alan."

"We're about to go down for dinner, the room's lovely. Oh, I'd better go. Alan's hungry."

"Enjoy your meal. Good night."

Picturing her friend, Freya sighed. Rose needed to slow her brain down and learn to relax. Freya thought back to her childhood. She'd learnt at an early age how to compartmentalise her thoughts, how to lock memories into a box and leave them there. It would help Rose if she could do the same, then she'd be more able to understand the messages and read the signs that were being sent her way. Meditation worked for her, she mused. Perhaps she could do some guided meditation sessions with Rose. Yes, she'd suggest that.

With the cottage ready and Nellie settled, it was now time to prepare herself. First, she ran a hot bath then dunked the muslin bag that she'd filled with fresh chopped herbs from the garden. The zingy aroma hit her nostrils and immediately began to permeate her lungs. Sage for purifying, rosemary for remembering, fennel for detoxing and her old favourites, lavender and chamomile to aid with relaxation. It was a strange blend, but she knew it was a concoction that had worked well for her in the past. Slowly, she immersed herself into the water which had taken on a greenish hue, her favourite colour. It felt warming and comforting, as though she'd found a place where she belonged at last.

As soon as she'd closed her eyes, images of rolling hills and green fields dotted with hedgerows infiltrated her brain. Birdsong soon followed as the experience intensified. Freya hadn't conjured up these visions in a meditation, they had been sent to her, but from where and why? The pictures continued like a film, as though she was a powerful bird flying low above the verdant countryside. Tiny cottages and small hamlets peppered the scene; it was beautiful, unspoilt. Freya somehow knew that she was in the past. There were no electricity pylons or motor vehicles, only a small horse and cart loaded with what looked like potatoes being driven by an older man with a young boy at his side. A rural idyl. Soon, the cart arrived at a rough building with a thatched roof; it looked like a small barn. The cart stopped in a cobbled yard where two young children were playing with a large hoop. A woman appeared in the doorway with a crying infant in her arms.

The sound of a dog barking in the distance infiltrated her vision. It seemed harsh, even abrasive, as though it was in a tunnel, somehow bouncing off the hard surfaces. The offensive noise was like a crescendo and brought Freya back. She opened her eyes to find Nellie at her side trying to get her attention. Startled, she sat up quickly causing some of the water to slosh onto the tiled floor. It was cold. Stone cold. And Freya was shivering. What time was it? How long had she been in the bath? This had never happened to her before.

Satisfied, Nellie returned to her bed by the patio doors and Freya vigorously rubbed herself dry with a warm towel, gradually feeling the sensation returning to her frozen limbs. She'd need to be more careful in future. The energy levels here were incredibly strong, seeping out of the old walls. No wonder Rose was constantly in a dither! It was almost too much. Was the cottage on an old lay line? That might explain it. She'd brought her divining rods; she'd have to investigate further tomorrow. But right now, she needed a hot drink which she took outside to catch the last of the sun's warming rays. Dusk was fast approaching.

The swirling, screaming swifts that had dominated the skies all day, were now being replaced by bats, the predators of the night sky. Freya could hear their high-pitched calls; she'd always been able to hear them, even as a child. She'd got exceptional hearing. It hadn't been unusual for her to stay awake all night, listening for tell-tale sounds in that draughty, Victorian building, not daring to fall asleep, envious of the bats as they left their roost in the roof void above her head. Unlike her, they were free. A shudder ran down her spine when she remembered being locked in one of the turrets after a beating. Isolated. Punished for telling such venomous tales. It had been a common occurrence at first, until she'd quickly learned to keep her mouth shut. Freya shook her head trying her best to dislodge the pitiful memory and placing it back in the locked box from which it had somehow managed to escape. Normally she was proficient at keeping them in. How she wished she could lose its key down a deep well forever.

22.

Escaping her past demons, Freya hurried back inside. It was nearly time. Her first task, after checking on Nellie, was to heave the old rocking chair into the study; it was difficult, but she managed. Freya had always been self-sufficient, independent. It was better that way. Methodically, she gathered the items that she felt were important, the box, the wedding ring and the old clay pipe, arranging them on the hearth next to the piece of damaged wood that contained his initials. It didn't look much, but it was all she had to work with. Next to them she added a homemade cake, a bowl of water, a pot of local honey, and a white candle - things that William would find familiar. Once she'd lit the candle, she sprinkled salt around its base then she cut two small squares of white paper and drew a pentagram on both of them. On one she wrote YES and on the other she wrote NO. Freya blew delicately on them, then placed one on each side of the flickering candle. But would it be enough? There was only one way to find out.

The one remaining task was to locate Rose's kimono. Rose was quite convinced that it possessed magical powers, but Freya was a little sceptical, knowing that it was Rose herself who possessed special qualities. It took a while to find the flimsy garment; she'd hidden it well, wrapped in a towel under the mattress on the spare bed. Genius. Alan would never think of searching there.

Back in the study, Freya walked around the rocking chair three times, inviting the spirits to join her, then made herself comfortable on its cushions in front of the hearth. She'd never seen William, but she felt sure she'd know him when he appeared. Nothing happened for a while, then the candle began to flicker. Freya felt sure someone was here. She could feel a cold chill in the room, just like Rose had described. This was it. Freya knew that this was her best chance to help solve the puzzle.

"Is anybody here?" she asked, trying not to over think the question.

Disappointingly, nothing materialised, so she tried again. "Is anyone with me tonight?"

Again, nothing, not a breath of air. Not one to give up easily, she had another go. "Does anyone want to join me this evening?"

Suddenly the candle flickered, it was slight but perceptible. "Is somebody here?" This time her voice sounded less confident. Was she nervous? Absolutely.

The candle's yellow flame leaned over to the right. Wow! It was leaning to the YES square. Astonished, she was both excited and anxious at the same time. She'd never had any success with this method in the past, she preferred Tarot cards, but they were open to interpretation, and she didn't want to get this wrong.

"Welcome. Is it William?"

Now perching on the edge of the chair, Freya gazed intently at the candle, but it remained upright, with not even a slight flicker.

"Am I communicating with William?"

Amazingly the small, yellow flame lurched over to the left. NO. Disappointment flooded through Freya. If it wasn't William, then who was it? Now confused, Freya was clueless. What should she ask next? She needn't have worried because instinct kicked in and she continued.

"Did you used to live in this house?"

Once more the flame answered YES. Freya couldn't remember the list of previous occupants that Rose had been able to rattle off, so she concentrated hard. William's wife, Anne. She was the next obvious choice.

"Thank you for coming. Is it Anne?"

After another short pause, the flame flickered to the right. Yes. It was Anne!

Freya was astonished and disappointed in equal measure; she'd wanted to talk to William, but Anne had materialised instead. There had to be a reason. Anne must have something important to tell her. But what?

"Have you got something you want to tell me?"

Again, the answer was YES. She was right, Anne had important news for her. But Freya was frustrated. She could only ask her questions that could be answered with a YES or NO. It was very limiting and was going to take a while. Anne couldn't tell her anything if Freya didn't ask the right questions. But what were they? What did she want to know?

"Have you got a message for Rose?"

The fame flickered but didn't lean in any particular direction which Freya found confusing, but she continued with her effort.

"Do you have a message for me?"

Immediately the light from the flame intensified burning much brighter for a few seconds before settling back down to a yellow glow. What did that mean? Freya decided to take it as a yes. But what could Anne possibly need to tell her? Now she was perplexed. A disturbing though materialised suddenly. Was Rose safe? Or was Anne trying to forewarn Freya of an imminent catastrophe? She needed to find out.

"Is Rose in danger?"

The answer was immediate. NO. Sagging, Freya sighed.

"Is Alan in danger?"

Again, it was a NO.

"Am I in danger?"

Another NO followed and Freya was relieved.

"So, if it's not danger, what is it? What do you want to tell me?"

At this point Freya stared in amazement as the little yellow flame danced in the darkness and grew taller while turning a deep shade of amber. Anne was clearly as frustrated as she was but how could she help her to get through? This method was obviously too limiting. She needed a Ouija board, but she knew never to use one alone, it always left you wide open to malevolent spirits. In fact, she had a deep apprehension towards Ouija boards; they could be dangerous to the inexperienced. But how else could she communicate with Anne?

Suddenly, the flame extinguished itself, leaving Freya sat alone in the darkened room. A draught of cold air swept through the space, causing something to fall off the desk behind her. Shocked, Freya tried to gather her thoughts. What had just happened? She needed time and a clear space to digest the experience. Slowly she looked around the room. Anne had gone. Reluctantly, she stood and ignited the smudge stick, once more wafting the aromatic smoke to cleanse and close the space where Anne had been. Under the rocking chair she retrieved the fallen item; it was a framed photograph of a young girl, with dark curly hair, tentatively holding a new-born infant on her lap. The little girl appeared to be perhaps three years old and seemed apprehensive of the baby in her arms. It must be Rose's daughters, Amy and Vicky. She'd never met them, but Rose spoke about them frequently. She clearly adored them both. An unpleasant thought creased her brow. Were Amy or Vicky in danger? How could she find out? Perplexed, she replaced the photograph back on the desk and went outside. She needed to think.

Outside, darkness had descended fully, and the inky sky was awash with stars, an astronomer's dream with little light pollution. But Freya's mind was too distracted to admire the constellations; she was desperate to figure out how to communicate with Anne. But her first task was to somehow find out if Amy and Vicky were safe. But how? Should she ring Rose? Probably not, it was almost midnight; she'd be fast asleep by now. No, she'd have to wait until morning.

Despite her frustrations Freya was exhausted and slept soundly. No sooner had she started out across the fields the next morning with Nellie, when her phone rang. It was Rose.

"Morning, how's Nellie? Did she sleep? Has she had her breakfast...?"

"Everything is just peachy. How was your night?"

Rose went on to describe her evening in great detail, but Freya was still wondering about Amy and Vicky and didn't know how to broach the subject.

"Have you heard from the girls?"

"Had a text from them both yesterday. It's weekend; they won't be up yet. Oh, Alan is eager to go down for breakfast, doesn't want to miss out. I'll ring back later."

Sighing, Freya looked over at Nellie who was happily trotting along the field margins. She was still no wiser about the girls. If anything was amiss, Rose would be the first to find out. And – it was only an educated guess that Anne was trying to communicate about them. Their photo falling onto the floor didn't necessarily signify danger. It could have been anything. Or even a coincidence. The only thing that was clear was that Anne had important news for her, and she needed to find out what before Rose returned. That only left two more nights. What should she do? A pitiful whining noise broke her train of thought. It was Nellie. Was she injured?

Striding as fast as she possibly could, Freya was soon beside the little dog who was frantically pawing at the grass on the side of a deep, waterlogged ditch. Once she was satisfied that Nellie was okay she peered into the matted vegetation in the bottom of the boggy trench. Something was moving. Was it a rat? Had Nellie caught a rat? She couldn't leave the poor creature to suffer, it was against her principles - she would have to retrieve it and finish it off. That would be the kindest outcome. Tentatively, Freya lowered herself into the ditch while Nellie looked on with interest. A dead branch from an overhanging tree steadied her until she heard a sharp crack, like splintering bone. It came away in her hand. Helpless, Freya tumbled into the soggy dyke and landed unceremoniously next to the poor creature. It stopped wriggling and froze. Freya gazed in amazement. Looking up at her out of the murky depths was a pair of blue eyes. Freya heaved a sigh of relief – she wasn't relishing the thought of being bitten by an injured rat. But what was it? Could it be a baby rabbit? Did they have blue eyes? Reaching into the mud Freya gently scooped the creature up and began untangling it from the wet vegetation cloaking its identity. A few moments later Freya gasped.

"Oh! Your poor little might!" It was a tiny kitten. Its blue eyes were open but one of them was clogged with a yellow discharge. "Let's get you home where I can have a good look at you."

Once the kitten was placed in her fleece pocket, she hauled herself out of the mire covered in stinky mud, to be met by Nellie who was eager to inspect her discovery.

"Good girl Nellie. Let's go and get cleaned up."

Back at the cottage, Freya stripped down to her

underwear and left her filthy clothes in the back garden then washed the worst of the mud off herself before retrieving the poor kitten from her muddy fleece. It stank.

"Let's get you cleaned up, shall we?"

Nellie sat patiently watching as Freya filled up a jug with warm water and began rinsing the frightened animal. It let out a pitiful mewl which Freya took as a promising sign. It was a fighter. When the worst of the mud was rinsed away, the kitten was placed in small bowl of warm water with a squirt of Nellie's dog shampoo and was given a careful bath. Now clean and smelling much better, Freya examined it carefully. It was all black except for one white paw and, mercifully, there didn't appear to be any injuries, but it had a nasty eye infection.

"It's straight to the vet with you, but we need a name. I wonder, are you a little girl or a little boy?"

A quick glance between its legs didn't answer her question. "You're too tiny for me to tell."

With the kitten now safely wrapped in a towel inside a shoe box, she found the number for the vet, who told her to bring it straight down.

A quick shower and a taxi ride later, Freya and the kitten were met by the vet nurse. "Thank you, we'll have a look at it. You can ring back later if you want to see how it's doing."

"What will you do with it?"

"Well, if it survives, we'll sent it to the local cat rescue. They have volunteers who hand rear them."

Nodding, Freya left the surgery and began the long walk to the bus stop, but after a while she stopped dead. It was fate. Meant to be. It was her kitten, and she would hand rear it. It had been found by her and Nellie for a reason. Turning around she was soon back at the surgery.

"Can I help you?" A friendly receptionist asked.

"Yes, I've just brought a kitten in that my friend's dog found – I want to keep it. Please."

"Just a minute."

Twenty long minutes later she was called in to find the kitten back in its box on a small heat pad.

"Good morning, and well done. Where did you find it? Were there any other cats about?"

"It was my Friends dog that noticed it in the bottom of a waterlogged ditch, it must have been crying. And no, I didn't see any other cats."

"It's one very lucky kitty."

"Is he okay? Can I take him home? How old is he?"

"Well, for a start it's a she, and she's about four weeks old. She's got an eye infection; I've started her on drops. She can't have been in the ditch for very long or her lungs would have had water and debris in them." Freya beamed at the news, but the vet wasn't finished. "She's taken a small feed just now, but the poor little thing is exhausted and needs to be kept quiet and warm."

"I can do that..."

The vet's face crinkled. "I'd prefer to keep her here overnight; it's quite a responsibility. She needs checking on every couple of hours and feeding until she gets her strength back. We need to make sure she doesn't develop a chest infection or anything nasty, but she's had some antibiotics and worming medication, so hopefully she'll be okay."

Freya's face dropped. "But it's Sunday tomorrow."

"Yes, come back on Monday morning..."

"I'd prefer to take her now please. I'll buy the feeding equipment from you. I can do it."

"If you're sure..."

"Absolutely!"

Armed with her little ball of fluff and all the equipment she needed; Freya climbed into the taxi on a mission. It was her kitten and wild horses wouldn't part her from it. It was fate. Meant to be.

23.

By the time she returned to the cottage, she had a missed call from Rose, but Freya's priority was to settle the new addition. It would need a bigger box. After searching in the shed for a while she came out triumphant with a plastic storage box that had been filled with plant pots. Freya gave it a thorough clean, lined it with a soft towel then opened the shoe box. A little head poked out from under the cover.

"Aww, hello sweetie. Aren't you a cutie!"

The ball of fluff let out a small mewl which grabbed Nellie's attention; she came trotting over and sat at the side of Freya, cocking her head to one side.

"Hi Nellie, you are a good girl." Freya reached into her pocket and gave her a treat. "Clever girl. Now you've got a new friend."

Again, Freya offered Nellie another treat, then put the empty shoe box on the floor. Puzzled, Nellie looked at it for a few seconds then picked up the small towel and dragged it away with her into her basket and curled up on top of it. Freya smiled and took it as a good sign. She hadn't known what to expect. Weren't dogs and cats supposed to be arch enemies?

The kitten took another small feed then was tucked back up on a hot water bottle to rest, leaving Freya free for a couple of hours. What should she do? Her first thought was her book of shadows. Taking it carefully out of her case, she read her last entry which she'd written on the summer solstice. It didn't contain any details that would help her communicate with Anne. But it was a weighty tome; she'd started it over twenty years ago and had been adding to it ever since. Did it contain any information or hints that would be of assistance? She couldn't remember. She'd diligently collected a wealth of material over the decades. Ever hopeful, Freya carried it into the study along with the box containing the sleeping patient and once more got comfortable on the old rocking chair.

Beginning at the very first entry Freya couldn't help noticing the difference in the style of her writing and how it had changed over the years. Page after page of spelling mistakes and grammatical errors jumped out at her; her dyslexia had been more of a problem back then, she remembered, as had her handwriting. She'd been born naturally left-handed but her malevolent carers at the convent where she'd lived and been educated as a child had rapped her on the knuckles with a wooden ruler whenever she used her left hand. When that failed to produce favourable results, her left arm was strapped securely behind her back, causing even more discomfort, but it had worked. Her once indecipherable handwriting had become more legible over time, and she'd learnt never to trust adults again, but at a great personal cost. She'd wished away her childhood years desperately longing for her sixteenth birthday so she could end her forced incarceration.

A loud meow broke into her memories it was the kitten; two blue eyes were trying to peer out of the box. Freya gently scooped her up into her arms and held her close to her chest. The kitten immediately began to purr.

"Oh my! You are feeling better little one. We need to find you a name. I'm sure something will come to me."

With the kitten now curled up snugly on her lap, Freya returned to her task, her book of shadows. It contained a wealth of information and experiences; many of the pages were battered and stained with remnants of herbs and candle wax. It was a precious resource with decades of spells, rituals, snippets from books she'd read, and important lessons learned alongside records of significant dreams and more. Surely she'd find something useful.

A short while later her head popped up. "Salem perhaps? No. I couldn't. You don't strike me as Salem."

Freya had been reading an entry that she'd made many years ago about the Salem witch trials in America in the sixteen-nineties when nineteen witches had been hung, many of them young girls and children. The evidence had all been spectral – with courtroom testimonies described by witnesses of the damage a witch's spirit had inflicted upon them. A travesty of justice!

The next article that piqued Freya's interest was about an injured hedgehog that she'd found hobbling down a lane in broad daylight. She'd contacted a rescue centre where they had amputated its damaged leg and like her new kitten, she'd taken it home, nursed it back to health; it had lived for four years in her enclosed courtyard. She'd called him Triceratops because of his three legs and spikey back. Freya put down her book and smiled. He'd been her familiar and had been sent to her for a reason. She felt sure that the few years that he'd been with her had been the most spiritually productive. He'd seemed to positively enhance her psychic ability, but that was over ten years ago. Freya glanced down at the sleepy ball of fluff on her lap. Definitely not a triceratops she mused.

Sighing, Freya leaned back and closed her eyes. It was way past lunch time, but she wasn't hungry; her mind was awash with questions and confusion. As she began to relax, she took a deep breath. What was that smell? It was a warm comforting smell, sweet and savoury at the same time. What was it? It hadn't been there earlier. Was it the kitten? Opening her eyes, she leaned down to sniff her new charge. Definitely not the kitten. As she raised her head, she saw the remnants of a curl of smoke dissipating into the air. Of course. It was pipe tobacco! Rose had told her about this phenomenon. It was William. Was he here?

"Hello. Is anybody there?"

"William, is that you?"

Edward struck four as a whisper of cold air brushed passed her cheek and ruffled a pile of papers on the desk behind her as it left the room. Freya was elated, but it was swiftly replaced with frustration. William had been. But what did he want? How could she find out?

Freya found her phone and decided to ring Rose; perhaps she'd have some ideas. It went straight to voicemail, probably no signal. Next Freya investigated the pile of papers on the desk. It felt wrong, as though she was snooping on her best friend, but it might provide some answers. They were notes from Rose's internet searches about the previous occupants of the house. The last entry was a couple of weeks ago when she'd found the engraved box containing the ring. William and Anne were listed as living here in 1860. Freya was certain that they were trying to tell her something, first the photo incident and now the papers. They had to be connected. She tried to ring Rose again, but got no reply. What was the connection? Freya spent a while collating the information that Rose had told her from her visions. Anne had been married to William but died in childbirth after managing to deliver her daughter first. Ethel was Anne's mother; they'd both been 'wise women' and midwives. Ethel took the baby to a local woman to nurse, then once weaned she was going to care for the child herself. What was the baby's name? Did she survive? That was where the trail went cold. Rose's laptop was on the desk next to the stack of scribbled notes, but Freya didn't know the password. As tempting as it was, she couldn't ask; that would be crossing a line.

24.

It was overcast on the banks of Loch Fyne. A heavy mist hung in the air, leaving a damp film on everything it touched. Rose hadn't noticed though; she was feeling somewhat guilty. If it wasn't for her, Alan wouldn't be in bed now, they'd be out exploring together. She'd persuaded him to try the oysters at lunchtime. She knew he wasn't a fan of fish, unless of course it was wrapped in a crispy, bubbly batter, but you couldn't visit Loch Fyne without sampling its famous oysters. Could you? She was okay, but poor Alan was laid up with a funny tummy. *"Go and explore on your own,"* he'd said. *"I'll be right enough in a couple of hours."*

So, after a short drive, here she was in her wellies, trekking through the soggy, bracken covered terrain following a rough path across a bleak Scottish hillside. Visibility was poor, but she was on a mission. At the top of the hill there was supposed to be the remnants of a stone circle; it was marked on the map. But the higher she climbed, the less she could see. She felt as though she was smothered in clouds. A few steps later, she caught her first tentative glimpse of a shape, a rough boulder with its edges softened by fog. Was this it, her destination? Picking up speed, she strode across to the stone. It was laid on its side covered in moss. She must be close. Striding on with renewed purpose, several ghostly shapes were gradually revealed, one by one.

The first stone was almost totally rounded, ground down by the relentless Scottish weather. The next one was taller and set off to one side. A sentinel. It stood proud as if it was the protector of all that it surveyed. More came into view; they were short and stumpy, resembling broken teeth set into a crooked jaw that was no longer able to chew. They all had one thing in common though, the fragile looking lichen that encrusted their surface, a hint to their great age. Together they were magnificent. Special. Totally mystifying. Rose hadn't noticed the few bedraggled sheep that were seeking shelter in their rain shadow. Nor did she detect the subtle change in the direction of the breeze as it swirled and twisted the fog in a clockwise direction around the perimeter of the ancient monument. It was only when the wind picked up and blew her hat off that she looked up at the sky. A circle of blue was opening up above her head. It grew increasingly wide, banishing the mist from around the stones. At last, Rose could see the circle in its entirety, perched on the summit of a rounded hill. The valleys below were still lost in the murk; there was nothing else visible except the stones encircling her and the cobalt blue sky above. She was above the cloud base. Was she in heaven? It certainly felt like it.

Lured by an unstoppable force, she was drawn to the smallest stone in the centre where she sat and let her fingers lazily trace a bizarre pattern hewn into the rock, a shallow cup surrounded by several concentric circles radiating out from it. What did it signify? Was it an ancient form of art or had it once served a purpose? A game perhaps, like marbles, to amuse the children. Rose thought not, it previously would have held great significance. She found herself pondering the mason who would have hammered out the pattern with his limited tools. What did this prehistoric human look like? Did he have a name? She was trying to imagine the type of clothes he would have worn when an eerie light caught her attention. Startled, she looked up and clutched her jacket tight to her body as if it were a suit of armour able to protect her from evil. Astonished, she blinked her eyes then screwed them tight shut, willing the light to disappear.

But when she opened them again it was still there. It was as though she was sat in an amphitheatre and a play was taking place around her. Except this wasn't Greece or Rome. No! She appeared to be sitting in the grounds of her cottage! But the gardens were much larger. Neither of her neighbour's houses existed; in fact, a lot of the village had disappeared. The rear half of her cottage sat on a large plot of land with an extensive vegetable patch and pretty orchard. There were several tumbling outbuildings with brown hens pecking about in a yard area. Suddenly, a young girl, aged about four years old, squealed while running out of an old wooden door leading from the kitchen, chasing a black and white collie.

"Lavinia! You know it's time to go back to Nana's house.

I've got work to do now."

The little girl pouted and flopped down at the side of the dog, tugging at its floppy ears. "I don't want to go Papa! I want to stay here with Meg! She's very special."

"I know, but you can come back to see Meg again tomorrow - if Nana lets you."

"But Papa… if I do one of my special wishes then you won't be able to find me."

The little girl promptly jumped up, closed her eyes and began to spin in a clockwise direction.

"No! Lavinia!"

Before she could finish her special wish, William rushed over, picked her up and spun her back in an anticlockwise direction. "You know that's forbidden, Lavinia!"

"Oh Papa! You are boring…"

A flash of white-hot light blinded Rose momentarily, and when her vision eventually returned, the fog had descended once more and William, Meg and Lavinia were nowhere to be seen.

Distracted by the buzzing of her phone Rose reached into her pocket; it would probably be Alan wondering where she was. She was wrong. It was Freya and she sounded excited.

"He's been! Rose, he's been - just now!"

Somewhat confused, Rose tried to get her head into gear. "What do you mean? Who's been?"

"William. In the study. I could see a curl of smoke and the same smell that you described."

Rose was even more perplexed. "Did you see him?"

"No, but I'm certain it was him."

"But... I've just seen him as well..."

The two friends spent the next twenty minutes comparing stories and discussing theories. William had made himself known to both women simultaneously. It was hugely significant, they declared. Once Rose returned home, they would decide together what to do next.

"One thing is certain," Freya declared. "It's another small piece of the jigsaw puzzle to slot into place."

It was turned six when Rose made it back to the hotel to find Alan in the shower. "Are you feeling better? Did you sleep well?"

"Back to my old self, but I did have a strange dream..."

"Really?" But Rose decided not to ask. She'd had enough weird encounters for one day.

25.

It was late when Alan and Rose returned from their break. Rose made a fuss of Nellie before meeting the new kitten.

"Has she got a name?" Rose enquired.

Freya beamed. "Yes. I've decided to call her Meg!"

"Oh! The same as Lavinia's collie?"

"Absolutely. Meg was probably Lavinia's familiar."

A crease crossed Rose's forehead. "What's a familiar?"

"Oh Rose!" Freya was a little exasperated with her friend. "It's a spirit, often embodied in an animal which is sent to guard and assist a person. Most witches have a familiar of some type."

"Oh, do I have one?"

"Of course. Nellie."

"Really?"

"Yes, really. You may not have noticed, but I expect she prompts you to do things."

"Oh yes, she reminds me when I've got a cake in the oven. She seems to know when they're ready."

Alan popped his head into the kitchen, halting their whispered conversation. "Are you ready to go Freya?"

Rose was quick to answer. "I think you've driven enough for one day. I'll run Freya home in the morning."

As soon as Alan had gone to work, the two women had a lazy breakfast together, going over everything they knew so far.

"So, what's the next step?" Rose asked.

"We need to find out what happened to William. Did he remarry? Where and when did he die? And Lavinia, did she go on to marry and have children? That could be your task on the website and parish records."

"Mm, it's not easy. Not everything was recorded accurately, and the writing is so hard to read. What are you going to do?"

"I need to find a way to communicate with Anne; she has a message for me."

"How will you do that?"

"Honestly – I'm not sure, but I'll think of something."

The rest of the week kept the two friends busy, Rose doing her research and Freya deliberating the possible ways to communicate with Anne's Spirit. The one idea that she kept returning to was the Ouija board. But it had to be safe, and she couldn't do it alone. Was Rose ready? Would she even agree to it? Freya knew it was a big ask. Where would they hold the session? The study at Rose's cottage was the obvious answer. But would that be wise? Surely it would be safer outside. And what about Alan? He'd definitely need to be out of the way. Frustrated, Freya sighed. A niggling doubt, deep inside, wormed its way into her head. The last time she'd used a Ouija board it had gone horribly wrong. A heavy downpour came from out of nowhere and caused her pretty courtyard to fill with water and flood her kitchen. It had taken ages to dry out afterwards. If that happened again, she felt sure she'd be evicted. No, she couldn't hold it in Rose's cottage; it was too risky.

Could Shona help? Possibly, but Freya didn't want to blow her cover. Freya knew that Shona was indeed a real wise woman, the ability had been passed down her family from mother to eldest daughter; it was traceable for generations. And she'd seen her at work. She was a true master. She'd even helped the police to solve several cold cases. Many years ago, they'd met by chance at Stonehenge. Had it been a coincidence? Absolutely not. But Shona didn't want to advertise her skills. Together, Shona and Freya had set up the small spiritual group in the hope that they might attract others. They had. Sadly, none of them had been real witches – just new age hippy types and young mothers looking for a diversion from their boring lives. But they were good people and Shona didn't turn them away. Inclusivity, that was one of the buzz words of their generation. They didn't practise any significant rituals or events at their meetings. No, it seemed they were destined to be just spiritual gatherings. It was also the reason why they didn't turn up to meetings at Freya's house anymore. She was too powerful. Things happened that had scared the others, unnatural things. Some members had left, and the remaining women largely avoided her except for pleasantries. Then Rose arrived. She'd been sent for a reason. Both Freya and Shona had known instantly. But why? Freya sighed, she was getting closer, she could feel it. Rose had arrived to navigate her. But to what? She had no idea. The only thing she was certain of was somehow it was connected to Anne. She needed answers. If that meant involving Shona then she would. But first she'd need to confess to Rose. She didn't want to offend her. That was the last thing she wanted. Rose had become a good friend; she was fond of her, and Freya knew that she needed her support. She was her mentor. Rose was also powerful, but she didn't know it. And power could also be dangerous. It was obvious that it was a newly acquired skill for Rose. She hadn't been coached in its use since birth like Shona or Anne and Lavinia. Pausing, Freya pondered for a while. Neither had she, but she'd always been aware of it. She'd known she was different. Was that why her mother had abandoned her into the merciless care system. She'd never know.

Shuddering, she closed that door with a resounding bang. She'd searched for years and found no trace of her. Clearly, she didn't want to be found. It had affected her more than she'd cared to admit. She knew it was the reason that she'd never previously succeeded in relationships. Abandonment issues, that's what it had said on her psychiatric report when she'd finally escaped care. What did they expect? Freya supposed most children who had navigated their way painfully through the care system would emerge with abandonment issues. The only relationship that had ever lasted had ended up being abusive and it had taken her a long time to recover from it. No, she was never going there again. Who needed a man anyway?

A tug on her trouser leg interrupted her memories. It was Meg. "Hello little one," Freya held the wriggling kitten up to her face. She was growing fast, a little ball of energy that liked nothing more than to chase a ball of scrunched up tinfoil around the house or pounce on a piece of string while Freya pulled on the other end. Meg took up a lot of Freya's time; she'd never had a real pet before, and she was smitten. She'd envied Rose's connection with Nellie, but now she had her very own Meg.

Freya's phone was on the chair at her side, she'd just been searching through a website about the use of Ouija boards when Meg pounced on it and began to pat at the screen. Freya laughed, "You little imp!"

"What? Why am I an imp? Freya, are you there?"

It was Shona.

"Oh! I'm so sorry Shona. Meg, my newly acquired kitten, appears to have rung you by accident."

Freya could hear Shona snort. "That would have been no accident. What's bothering you Freya?"

"Erm, well, it's complicated."

"I'm on my way."

Shona sat back and listened patiently while Freya recounted the story from beginning to end.

She'd known about Rose's visions, connected to the antiques she'd purchased, but Freya hadn't previously told her about the rocking chair or William and Anne.

"Wow!"

"Yes. Wow!"

Clasping her hands on her lap, Shona gave the subject her full attention. "Have you tried scrying?"

"Oh, yes. I forgot that bit — I've tried tasseography."

"And?"

"Mm, I think I may have got my wires crossed — I sat in the rocking chair but was holding the candlesticks. It was supposed to be about the candlesticks but most of the energy came from the rocking chair."

"As it would."

"Yes. But I didn't realise that at the time."

"Runes or tarot perhaps?"

"I've tried that too but alone in my courtyard." Freya crinkled her freckled nose. "It was a bit vague."

"It seems whatever we do it needs to be at Rose's cottage."

"Agreed, but what?" Freya sighed.

The two women sat and pondered in silence, but Freya had already come to the obvious conclusion.

"I know what you're thinking." It was Shona who broke the pregnant pause, her eyes widening. "Ouija board."

"It had crossed my mind."

"Do you think Rose is ready? It's exceptionally powerful. I think I'd prefer to start with a séance."

Disappointed, Freya shrugged, but Shona continued regardless. She was, after all, their leader. "I know you've tried on your own, but three is a much better number."

So, it was agreed. Freya would try to break the news as

gently as possible to Rose then they would organise a séance.

26.

Alan was flummoxed. What had he done wrong? Rose had hardly said a word since he'd got home from work, and there hadn't been a pudding. She knew how much he loved his puddings. Perplexed, he gave it some thought while he tidied his tools away and put the dust cover back over his beloved Giulia 1750 GTV. Was it him? Rose had seemed so much better since their little break away, he mused. There previously non-existent sex life had even improved. But now it seemed she was back in her rut. How could he help? Was it something to do with her friend? Glancing around the garage for a final check, before he pressed the button to lower the door, he stopped. Was it a lover? Had they fallen out? Was that why their sex life had improved? He shuddered. What now? They needed to talk. And soon. But how would he broach the subject? Holding his head high, he opened the back door into the utility room. Now. He'd talk to her now. They could get over this, couldn't they? All marriages had sticky patches, didn't they? But not their marriage. Rose had always been there for him. In fact, he couldn't remember any problems, apart from sleepless nights when the girls were babies. But that was normal, wasn't it? Yes, he thought. No time like the present. They would discuss this now. Knock it on the head. He'd even make their bedtime drink tonight.

"Rose," he shouted, "tea or hot chocolate?"

But there was no reply. He'd make tea; hot chocolate was a bit heavy for a warm evening. Or would she prefer a glass of cold Pinot Grigio? That might help. He took a long gulp as he carried the glasses into the lounge. Cold and zesty. Perfect.

"Rose, I thought..."

Alan halted in his tracks; she wasn't here. His wife wasn't here! He discarded the glasses on the mantle shelf and headed into the study. No. And there was no sign of her in the kitchen or dining room either. Perhaps she'd gone to bed already? But no, she wasn't in any of the bedrooms or bathrooms. Now what? He'd just come through the back garden, and it was empty. That only left the front. Relieved, he could hear her voice in the distance, but who was she talking to? Was it a man? Slowly, he crept nearer, staying close to the hedge.

Rose sighed. "Yes, I know, but you could have told me sooner."

Frustratingly, Alan couldn't hear any of the responses, only Rose's words.

"I do understand. I just feel a little, well, betrayed."

...

"Okay, perhaps that's a little too strong."

...

"Of course, I forgive you – we're a team and I do get the secrecy."

...

"Oh, don't worry about Alan, he'll never suspect. Anyway, he's always in the bloody garage."

...

"Yes, we can do it when he's at work."

...

"No, I agree, it would definitely freak him out."

...

"Okay, I'll give it some thought. Yes. Bye, I'll call you tomorrow."

...

Rose hung up and sat back on the garden bench while Alan, hurt and confused, scurried back inside. He was in the lounge gulping down the second glass of wine when she eventually came back in, and Rose thought he looked a little odd.

"I didn't know you were here. I'll put the kettle on…"

"Don't bother, I've had wine." He couldn't bring himself

to look into her face so he stared out of the window while he continued. "As you can see, I've had a couple of glasses of wine, so you might want to sleep in the spare room. I always snore after wine."

The empty wine glasses were abandoned and he strode past her without saying another word.

Staring at his back as he left the room, Rose wondered what on earth had come over him. This wasn't like him at all. In fact, she'd thought that they were getting on better now since their little break. What could possibly have upset him? Or was it who? Had he fallen out with someone? It couldn't have been work related; he'd seemed fine when he came home. And she hadn't done anything wrong. No. Whatever, or whoever had upset him had happened this evening. Was it his mistress? Was he planning to leave? How would she cope? What would they tell the girls?

Both Rose and Alan, in their separate bedrooms, tossed and turned, each doubting the other until dawn.

When Rose appeared for breakfast, Alan had already left. His dirty dishes were in the bottom of the sink and he'd left a scribbled note.

Something's come up, I'll be working late.

There wasn't even a kiss. They always added a kiss to the bottom of their notes. This must be serious, Rose decided, and it probably wasn't anything to do with work. What could have possibly gone wrong at work in the middle of the night? Very infrequently, when they had heavy lifting gear on site or a road closure, he might be needed, but she wasn't aware of anything, and he'd always tell her beforehand if there was a possibility that he'd be called away to a site meeting. No. She was certain this wasn't work related. It had to be his mistress. What should she do? Her thoughts shattered into a million pieces, like light passing through a prism.

Wandering around aimlessly, Rose felt lost, and the cottage felt empty. Should she ring the girls? Nellie appeared at Rose's side, rubbing against her leg as if sensing her distress, adding a quiet whimper.

"Do you want to go for a walk?"

Nellie responded with a yap, so Rose set off across the fields; it gave her space and time to think. After half a mile and a few long deep breaths later, she'd made a decision. She wouldn't involve their daughters. It wasn't their problem, and they didn't need to know. She had no physical evidence that Alan was having an affair. No. She wouldn't upset their girls without hard evidence.

On her return, her first task was a thorough search of the cottage. She began in their bedroom, meticulously going through all of Alan's pockets but she found nothing except several receipts. None of them were for flowers or expensive jewellery; they were mainly from garages for brake fluid and engine oil. His bedside drawers contained nothing of interest, neither did his shelves. Her next thought was the study, but again she found nothing in his desk. Next she took all of his car books from the bookshelf and leafed through them. It took her over an hour, but again she came up with nothing! Disheartened, her eyes landed on his laptop. She'd never touched it before. Was that a step too far? Rose sat with her head in her hands. She needed to know. With renewed enthusiasm, she turned the machine on. It asked for a password. What could it be?

"Think Rose, think!" she shouted into the still room.

She knew he was predictable, so she tried the obvious, date of birth. No. That didn't work. His mother's maiden name. No. That didn't work either. She suspected that she only had one more attempt then it would probably lock her out or send a traceable email, or something along those lines. She couldn't risk that. Beyond frustrated, she made a strong black coffee and sat outside. Once her cup was drained, she sat back, her eyes landing on the garage. His cars! Of course! But what were they called? He had three Alfa Romeos, each one slightly different. Which should she choose? Did he have a favourite? She'd never asked.

Back in the study she sat in the rocking chair with his laptop on her knee and closed her eyes asking for divine intervention. When she opened them, she'd made up her mind. Slowly and deliberately, she typed the words carefully. Alfa Romeo, then held her breath. It worked!

She'd finally got access to his emails. A feeling of guilt descended rapidly. Was it wrong? Yes, it was wrong, but it was also necessary.

Rose was again flummoxed, he had three email addresses! Why did he need three? Methodically, she set about her task, starting with his work account, but there was nothing of interest, just work-related issues; there were thousands of them and after the first thirty or so she closed it down. Next was the address that she was familiar with. It took her half an hour to go through the first one hundred, but most were about cars or motor sport events that he was either attending or helping to organise. None of them appeared to be from women either. On to the last account. This was more interesting. It appeared to be the address that he used to order things. Her new laptop was here, as were countless car parts and products, but nothing suspicious. Deflated, she sat back. What now?

An incoming text distracted her; it was Freya.

Are you free to talk?

Rose immediately rang her back.

"Hi Rose, I didn't know if you'd want to talk to me after my confession last night."

"Of course, we're friends. It just took me a while to get my head around it."

"What are you doing today?"

Rose went on to tell her about Alan and her ongoing search.

"Have you looked in his internet browser history?"

"No, how would I do that?"

Freya talked her through the process and Rose was totally shocked with what she found.

"Oh my God!" Rose held her hand over her mouth, speechless!

"What have you found, Rose. Are you okay?"

Stunned, Rose eventually found her voice. "Freya, his last search was *How do I find out if my wife is having an affair?*"

Freya burst out laughing and took a while to compose herself. "I'm sorry Rose."

"It's not funny! He thinks I'm having an affair! Imagine that. Me! Having an affair! As if!"

"Is there anything else? Anything incriminating?"

"I'll ring you back."

The next twenty minutes of Rose's time was spent searching through his recent history. Car stuff, and more car stuff. Forums, lots of them, again mainly car forums but some photography ones too, she'd forgotten that he was keen on photography. He'd taken lots of photos when they were up at Lock Fyne. They were very good. He was going to have one in particular enlarged and framed, a view looking down the loch with mist and cloud swirling around the mountains in the distance. It was stunning. Photos! Of course, he might have a picture of this elusive woman. A short while later she'd managed, with Freya's help, to access his photos but again it was images of his cars at various events as well as the photos from their recent break. The only woman in any of the images was her!

Nothing, she'd found nothing. Was she being silly? The only place left to search was his garage. But by teatime she'd found nothing. Not a scrap of evidence to suggest he was having an affair. Perplexed, she rang Freya.

"Well, that's a good thing, isn't it?"

"Yes and no."

"Explain."

"Why is he being so weird?"

"Well, have you thought that it's you that's being weird, and he's just as confused as you?"

Rose hadn't. "Mm"

"I'm not surprised Rose, there's such a lot going on. We need to get to the bottom of this mystery, but I have to warn you, it won't be easy."

"It seems nothing ever is."

Freya could picture her friend sat in the old rocking chair and felt sorry for her dilemma. "Leave Alan be for now. Have you heard from him?"

"A brief text saying he's been called to a site meeting and will be away for a few days. It's not unusual, it happens a couple of times a year, but he normally tells me a day or two in advance."

"Well, it's probably a good thing that he's out of the way for a while; it will give us some space. Let's do the séance tomorrow night. You need to prepare; it's going to take its toll."

27.

Shona stepped through the front door and smiled. "Thank you for hosting this special meeting."

Freya followed her in and hugged Rose. "Are you ready?"

Nodding, Rose showed the pair into the kitchen where she'd prepared a special herbal brew for them to consume. Shona sat with her eyes closed and her head bent forward with a myriad of expressions creasing her youthful features. Once their cups were empty, Shona stood up unexpectedly. Gone were the air kisses and pleasantries, this was a whole different Shona. In fact, Rose thought that she hardly recognised her anymore.

"I'm going to look around."

Startled, Rose jumped up. "Oh, I'll show you the…"

Freya put her hand on Rose's shoulder. "Let her go alone."

A short while later, they heard Shona's voice. "Yes, it's strongest in here, but it's reasonable in the kitchen too."

Rose was unsure what was reasonable, so she jumped up to investigate. Shona was in the study, facing the old fireplace, she then turned abruptly and pushed the desk back to the wall and began issuing instructions. "Take all gadgets out, laptops, phones and iPads. Oh, and cover that cabinet with a sheet. Then pull the curtains across the window."

Rose couldn't imagine why they needed to do these things, but she did as instructed anyway.

Freya had been tasked with collecting together the items they would need. Rose watched on in silence, feeling a little redundant while her friend set up an altar on the old brick hearth, white candles, homemade bread, a jug of milk, a jar of local honey and a few small pieces of wood.

"What is the wood for?" Rose asked innocently.

"It's Palo Santo, holy wood." Shona's reply was short and sharp.

Freya looked at Rose apologetically. "Shona frequently becomes irritable before commencing a project. I'm the polar opposite; I prefer to achieve a zen like state."

"Well, I feel a bit stressed," Rose admitted, biting her lower lip.

Freya took her hand. "The wood is cedar. We'll burn it in the fire for a few minutes and once it gets going, we'll extinguish it."

"Won't there be a lot of smoke? The chimney has been taken down."

"Yes, that's the plan. Cedar cleanses the room and helps to entice the spirits. Especially William, he will be attracted to wood."

Rose was momentarily glad that Alan was away on-site somewhere; he'd be furious if he knew they were about to fill his study with smoke. Freya left Rose in the study watching Shona, then returned with a small cat carrier. Inside, Little Meg was curled up asleep.

Once again, Rose looked questioningly at Freya, desperately hoping there wasn't going to be any sort of sacrifice and was now beginning to feel rather uncomfortable. Was this really such a good idea? She hoped that Shona knew what she was doing.

"Okay, we're ready. Go and get Nellie." It was Shona, issuing orders again.

Rose wasn't comfortable involving her beloved pet, but Shona gave her a hard stare, so she quickly obliged. Once the five of them were in the study, Shona closed the door. Nellie began sniffing around the cat carrier and little Meg opened her eyes, stood up, stretched and yawned. Freya unzipped the front of the carrier, allowing Meg her freedom. Rose held her breath, her eyes darting to Nellie. How would she react? Nellie sniffed at the little cat and nudged her with her nose. Meg responded by patting Nellie's nose with her one white paw then they sat down together. By now, Freya had ignited the candles and the small pieces of wood and Shona was sitting upright in the old rocking chair in front of the hearth. Her chin dropped forward onto her chest and she emitted a bizarre moan while emptying her lungs. Anxiously, Rose stared at her. She had no idea what to expect and was beginning to feel afraid.

"Close your eyes and take a few deep breaths. Think about Anne, William and Lavinia," Freya whispered softly.

Rose tried, but smoke was now filling the room and her lungs. Freya blew the small fire out, which caused even more smoke; Rose was now coughing and her eyes were beginning to sting. "We need to open the window! Get the animals out!" she shouted.

"No!" Shona's head popped up. "Someone's here!"

The hairs on the back of Rose's neck stood on end and a prickling sensation rapidly spread across the surface of her body. It was quite uncomfortable. She glanced across the smoke-filled room to Freya for reassurance, but her friend also appeared to be struggling. This was unlike anything Rose had experienced previously. Her other visions and dreams hadn't caused her to feel distressed before, only a little confused. Rose didn't like it at all.

Panicking, fearing they were all going to choke to death, she darted for the door and opened it wide reaching for Nellie and Meg. Rose managed to get the two pets to safety before everything went black. Rose had fainted.

When she woke all the doors and windows were open and Nellie was at her side, licking her cheek. Groggily, Rose sat up and rubbed her eyes. Once they began to focus, she could see Freya offering her a glass of cold water.

"Rose, thank goodness. I was about to ring for help. How are you feeling?"

Now in a sitting position, she took the offered drink and gulped it down. "Oh, I needed that."

Freya helped her up and guided her into the back garden. "Take some deep breaths. You need some fresh air."

"Is everyone else okay? What about the animals?"

"Thankfully, everyone's fine." Freya put her hand on Rose's shoulder and continued. "I'm so sorry, that didn't go as planned. We didn't even get a chance to open the circle; it appears someone is very eager to communicate with us."

Rose scowled. "I did warn you that the chimney had been removed."

"I know and I'm sorry, but usually there isn't that much smoke. That wasn't normal."

Rose rolled her eyes. "Freya, I don't think any of this is normal!" Agitated, she stood up and walked across the garden to stroke Meg, who was curled up enjoying a patch of warm sunshine. "Anyway, what happened? Who was there? And where's Shona?"

"I'm here," Shona popped her head out of the back door.

"Did you manage to communicate with anyone?" Rose enquired.

Sighing, Shona walked out into the garden. "They were definitely here, but sadly I didn't get chance to ask any questions. They left as soon as you burst out of the door. If only you hadn't..."

Rose couldn't believe what she was hearing. "Shona! If I hadn't then we'd all now be in hospital suffering from smoke inhalation!"

Waving a dismissive arm, Shona disagreed. "Nonsense, the smoke was clearing. Now we'll have to do it all over again."

"Not a chance – not in my house anyway! And no more Palo Santo, or whatever it was called."

Freya put herself between the two women to prevent any further disagreement. "I think we've all had enough for one day." She walked towards Shona and continued, "come on, let's go and leave Rose to rest and we can think about what to do next."

Rose was relieved to be alone again. Thankfully, the smoke had cleared and she was now feeling much better so decided to go for a walk with Nellie. Once out in the open countryside, Nellie turned left into a small woodland, an area that they hadn't explored previously. For good reason - Rose read the large sign. PRIVATE. KEEP OUT. Clearly, Nellie couldn't read. Shouting after her mischievous pup, Rose hurried on behind, trying to keep up with Nellie as she scampered about, investigating the numerous rabbit holes hidden in the undergrowth. Suddenly, Rose stopped dead in her tracks next to a patch of vibrant green nettles on top of a small mound beneath the shade of two mature oak trees. A cold, eerie feeling washed over her. Rose didn't like it one bit. A shiver radiated down her spine from the tip off her head right down to her toes. It felt unnatural. Spooked, she called for Nellie who came scampering over. Once at her side Nellie whimpered.

"Can you feel it too?"

Rose didn't wait for an answer, turning quickly. Nellie followed her and they both burst out into the sunshine and headed for home.

As soon as she entered the cottage, she could smell the acrid tang of smoke. She threw all of the windows and doors wide open, desperately hoping that the smell would have gone in time for Alan's return, whenever that was going to be. She'd sent him a text earlier, but he still hadn't replied.

Later that day, Rose did receive a text. Was it from

Alan? No, it was from Shona.

Are you feeling better?

Rose wasn't sure she wanted to talk to Shona at the moment, but she didn't want to appear rude either.

Yes, I'm okay now. Went for a walk and had a quiet afternoon in the garden.

Good, next time I think we will have to do it outside.

Rose wasn't convinced that there was going to be a next time, but kept that thought to herself.

28.

Alan had already spent two nights in a local bed and breakfast and was fed up with the lukewarm breakfast buffet on offer. The pre-packed sandwiches that he'd purchased for his lunches had been abysmal and the choices from the two takeaways in the nearest small town weren't much better either. And to make matters worse - the bed was lumpy too. He was thoroughly miserable. But most of all, he missed Rose. It was now occurring to him that perhaps he'd been spoilt for all of these years, coming home to his favourite dinners every evening not to mention his packed lunches made from homemade bread and fresh, homegrown salads. Was it time to go home to his wife? Perhaps. He'd told her he was away on-site, but here he was sat in a dingy room only a few miles away from his clean, comfortable bed. And Rose. His world and his life. But his mind continued to flip from one thought to another. His dilemma. Was she having an affair? He had to admit it would be way out of character for her. He'd always trusted her implicitly. But – he had overheard **that** phone call! Who had she been talking to? What were her exact words now? He tried to recall them.

"Oh, don't worry about Alan, he'll never suspect, anyway, he's always in the bloody garage."

Cocking his head to one side, he looked into the scratched, dressing table mirror. "Am I always in the garage?" he asked himself.

He quickly came to the conclusion that yes, he probably was. Then there were the other two alarming comments he'd overheard.

"Yes, we can do it when he's at work."

And.

"No, it would definitely freak him out."

What exactly could they do when he was at work? Who were they? And what would freak him out? He was perplexed. He'd used one of the spare company cars and had sat in the village opposite their house several times over the last two days and nights, but he'd witnessed nothing unusual. Freya had called with another woman, but they hadn't stayed very long. There was nothing suspicious about that, except the other woman was wearing rather strange clothes. Rose had been out for walks with Nellie, but that was all he'd seen. No men. He'd even taken Rose's wildlife camera and positioned it in the drive facing the cottage, but when he'd checked it this morning, no one except the post man and the milk man had been. There was no access from the rear of their property as it backed on to the small village school, so no one could have sneaked in that way. Flummoxed, he laid back down on the uncomfortable bed, staring at the yellowed ceiling, wondering what to do next. Rose had texted him several times, but his replies had been brief and curt.

Had he got this completely wrong? It could have just been an innocent phone call about anything. After all, he'd got no proof. Nothing to go on. Was he being stupid? The problem was he didn't know, and he couldn't ask anyone. What should he do? Having woken up with back ache yet again from the lumpy, uncomfortable bed in the early hours, he'd made his mind up. He'd go home after work today. He'd do a bit of snooping. Yes, he'd look through her things to see if he could find anything suspicious. He felt a little better now that he'd made a decision.

Rose appeared startled when he breezed into the kitchen at six-thirty. "Oh, I wasn't expecting you for dinner, I've had mine."

Trying to act normally, he leaned in to give her his customary peck on her cheek. "No worries, I'm sure you'll come up with something." Turning he added, "I'm going for a shower. That should give you enough time."

Bristling, Rose sighed, he hadn't changed one bit – but what did she expect, a miracle? When he reappeared, he felt much fresher and sat down to double egg and chips. The eggs were cooked to perfection, the yellow was golden and runny, and the whites had a slight crispiness at the edges – just as he liked them. He thought back to his breakfast earlier that morning and shuddered. A poached egg that would have broken the window if he'd thrown it and the toast was like soggy cardboard. No, he decided. He was better off with Rose – no matter what she was up to. He felt sure they could come to an understanding. He wasn't throwing thirty-seven years of happy marriage in the bin for anything or anyone. He was staying. They'd work it out.

Their normal routine continued until Saturday morning when Rose expected him to rush into the garage after breakfast, but he didn't.

"What are your plans today?" he asked cheerily.

"I'm meeting Amy and Vicky at an antique fair. I thought you'd be away."

"No, I decided not to do this weekend's event – think I need a rest after being away for a few days."

Leaning forward Rose took his hand. "Yes, you do look tired. You can come with us if you like."

Alan shook his head, "No, you go and have a nice day with the girls – give them my love. Think I'll put my feet up for a change and read."

He watched Rose's car leave the drive and his shoulders sagged. Where should he begin? Pouring himself a strong coffee he decided on their bedroom. Carefully he emptied her drawers, making sure that he returned every item in the exact same order so she wouldn't notice. His search was futile. Next, he moved on to her wardrobe looking through any pockets and bags before progressing onto her shelves. But still he found nothing. His search of the spare room was fruitless too; there was nothing of interest in the small wardrobe or chest of drawers. But Alan hadn't thought to look under the mattress where Rose kept her dream diary and kimono.

What next? He stood and scratched his chin. The kitchen. Yes, he hardly ever went in the kitchen cupboards apart from the one containing the baking and biscuit tins. With renewed enthusiasm, he looked behind packets and tins then progressed to jars of pungent smelling herbs. What did she use these strange things for anyway, he mused? He felt sure he'd know if anything that smelled so strong and unpalatable was in his food. Confused he read the labels. Chamomile, Sage, Thyme – yes he'd heard of those but Mugwort, Pennyroyal and Patchouli. What on earth were they for? Sighing, he thought back over their many years together. She'd always been a bit alternative, frequently trying things like aromatherapy oils on minor ailments, and they'd usually helped. Yes, he thought, nothing suspicious here. So, he meticulously replaced the jars back in their places. No, he'd found nothing of interest in the kitchen.

Soon, his attention was focused on the dining room. A bowl of pleasant-smelling potpourri was nestled on the sideboard next to a group of candles and a few decorative stones. Moving on, he emptied the drawers in the sideboard, but they only contained more candles and pebbles. Rose had always enjoyed collecting shells and pebbles with the girls when they were on holiday, perhaps they were sentimental items. Nothing. He'd come across nothing again. No unfamiliar bottles of perfume or pieces of jewellery that could have been a token from a lover. No cards or hastily scribbled love poems. He sat down, his body sagging. That was a good thing, wasn't it? But, he still hadn't got an answer to his dilemma. Who had she been talking to on the phone? Frustrated, Alan sighed, the only place left was the study. But that was largely his domain. Apart from the newly restored fireplace, Rose had never taken an interest in the study. It wasn't looking promising.

The first thing that hit him when he entered the study was the acrid smell. Smoke. Had Rose tried to have a fire? No, surely she wouldn't have done something so stupid – she knew the chimney had fallen down and had to be removed. He strode over to the window and opened it wide, and his mind suddenly wandered back to the strange night when he'd found her on the floor in this very room. Was it a coincidence? The details were gradually coming back to him, it was just after the chimney incident, and she had claimed that she was removing yet more dust. And just as she had opened the window to shake the duster outside, a flash of lightning had hit the cottage. Yes, he'd been extremely concerned and was about to call an ambulance, but she'd convinced him otherwise. What was it about this room? His eyes surveyed every corner then landed on the desk. There was a pile of papers next to Rose's laptop. What had she been writing? Slowly, he sank into the swivel chair and picked them up. They were notes that she'd made about this William chap that had lived here a couple of centuries ago. Yes, that's right, she'd shown him the ring in the carved box that the young joiner had found. He carried on reading but soon got bored. It was nothing but lists of names and dates along with occupations of the predecessors of this building. They were all long dead and weren't relevant to his inquiry. Next he lifted the lid of Rose's laptop but felt a twinge of guilt. He wouldn't want Rose to look through his gadgets; they were personal in a weird kind of way. Was it wrong? Yes, he thought it probably was, but he was going to look anyway. There might be incriminating emails! He knew all of Rose's passwords; she was hopeless when it came to technology, and he'd had to set everything up for her. His mind stilled, there weren't many things she was hopeless at though. They were a great team. He helped her and she looked after him. Wasn't that how it was supposed to be? Continuing, he noted that her emails contained little of interest. Most of them were from Amazon trying to get her to purchase more items that she didn't need. There were some from the bank, a couple from a gardening website that she'd got her seeds from and two from charities that she subscribed to. Nothing incriminating. This was proving more difficult than he'd first anticipated. Feeling like a spy, he opened her browsing history, but to his amazement it contained nothing. He felt sure that she must have searched the world wide web recently. Everyone did! Surely, Rose wouldn't know how to clear her browsing history – unless someone had shown her. He hadn't. Was it one of the girls? And why would she want to, unless she had something to hide? Now Alan felt even more confused. What had Rose got to hide?

The sound of the front door startled him; Rose was back. What time was it? Quickly closing her laptop, he grabbed a car book from a shelf and sat back.

"Have you had a successful day?" he asked when she popped her head around the door.

"I didn't find much, just a few pots for the garden. I'm desperate for a cup of tea. Oh, and the girls send their love."

Alan helped her take the galvanised pots into the garden then Rose put the kettle on. After dinner, they chose a film and sat down together but Alan couldn't concentrate; he couldn't understand why she'd deleted her browsing history.

29.

On Monday morning, Rose set off into the countryside with Nellie. Once off her lead, she bolted across the field to the small patch of private woodland. Exasperated, Rose shouted while running as fast as she could behind the naughty pup. When she arrived out of breath, she leaned against one of the old trees to recover while her eyes darted around. Where was Nellie? Rose couldn't see her.

"Nellie! Nellie! Where are you? Come back!"

But Nellie wasn't listening; she was too busy digging down a disused badger set. Now concerned, Rose began to search through the shrubby undergrowth before arriving near the small mound. Once again, the hairs on the back of her neck began to prickle and an achingly cold sensation consumed her. Feeling more than a little uncomfortable she backed away. That's when she heard the noise, a scratching sound. It was close. Could it be Nellie?

"Nellie! Is that you?"

Nellie didn't answer. But in her peripheral vision Rose saw earth being thrown into the air near a deep hole beneath the mound. Bending down, she sighed and tried to peer inside.

"There you are, come out at once!"

Nellie obliged and burst out into the sunshine feeling very pleased with herself. She had an object in her mouth. What was it? At first Rose was alarmed, was it a badger kit?

"Nellie, give!"

Normally, Nellie would have obeyed her instantly. But not today; she wasn't about to relinquish her buried treasure. It was hers!

"Nellie!" Rose continued to chase her errant pet through the trees until they came out onto the lane. She was now frantic and managed to grab her collar. Nellie dropped the object and sat down, cocking her head to one side in a quizzical manner. Relieved, Rose sighed and her shoulders sagged. It was only an old bone. But when she bent down and held the object in her hands, relief was quickly replaced by dread! It wasn't any old bone; it was a lower jawbone, and it was human. Her mind was transported back to the early eighties when she was a student nurse, sitting in her anatomy class. She'd loved anatomy. The human body and its physiology had always fascinated her. Yes, this was a human mandible. It was quite small and more pointed so had probably belonged to a female. Nellie barked, bringing Rose back from the early eighties. The same cold feeling flowed through her like a wave. What should she do now? Her first thought was Alan; she'd ring Alan; he'd know what to do. But his phone went to voicemail, so she rang his assistant.

"Sorry, he's out of the office, gone to a meeting. Is it urgent?"

"No, I'll try later."

After hanging up, she sat down on the dusty lane and put her head in her hands. What should she do now? Who had it belonged to? Was it a crime scene? Logic slowly returned. It was probably just a woodland burial; they were quite popular now. Eco friendly. Yes, that would be it. Should she just put the bone back and walk away? It was tempting. Yes. That's what she'd do. Turning back, she retraced her steps, approached the menacing hole and shuddered; it felt like an entrance to the dark world of the underground. Reaching in, she placed the bone as far inside as she could then stepped back. There. Nobody would ever know. She'd never been very religious, but she apologised for her naughty pup and asked for forgiveness. Once more she reappeared into the sunshine, but Nellie wasn't happy. The little dog turned tail, rushed back to the hole and retrieved the bone, dropping it at Rose's feet.

"Oh, Nellie! You are so naughty!"

Sighing, Rose was perplexed. She needed to think, so she sat down once more on the dusty lane to consider her options. If Nellie could get the bone so easily then so could scavenging animals, foxes and badgers, then the remains could end up scattered around the countryside. That wasn't a nice thought. If she'd buried her loved one in a woodland, she wouldn't like that idea one bit. No, she had no choice, she had to inform someone, but whom? Glancing about, she saw the familiar farmhouse in the distance. Yes, the farmer would know what to do; in fact, it was probably his grandmother or some other relative. Decision made. Rose carried the bone down the lane and continued to the farmhouse. Knocking on the heavy wooden door she stepped back and waited. No one answered, so she tried again. Several minutes later, she turned and poked her head into a few of the outbuildings, but nobody was around. Should she leave the bone on the doorstep? Common sense prevailed and Rose decided against that. No, she had no choice, she'd have to call someone, but whom? She'd found human remains. At last, she'd decided, she'd needed to ring the police.

Rose retrieved her phone and an image of her friend popped into her head. Yes, she'd ring Freya first.

"Hi Rose, are you okay? You sound a bit stressed."

It took Rose a few minutes to get the story out, but she felt better now that she'd told someone. And Freya agreed, she needed to ring the police. In fact, she was already climbing on her bike and would be with her soon.

The police however took a little more convincing.

"Don't worry, dogs excavate bones on a regular basis. It's probably an old animal bone – they usually are. Seen it lot's 'o times."

Rose wasn't happy and felt as though she was being patronised, despite her telling them more than once that she'd been a nurse and was convinced it was human.

"I'll tell you what, take it home with you and I'll ask an officer to call in sometime today."

Now frustrated, Rose slipped the bone into her bag and strode home to find Freya stood on her doorstep.

Rose accepted a much-needed hug from her friend. "How are you feeling, it must have been quite a shock. What did the police say?"

Over strong coffee, the two women carefully examined the jawbone and Freya agreed that it was probably human. Before wrapping it in tissue, they held a small blessing ritual then placed it in a shoe box and put it on a shelf in the kitchen out of harm's way. They spent some time discussing Rose's progress - or lack of it, searching the ancestry website for more information about William and Anne. By late afternoon, Freya had left, and Rose was alone again with her thoughts. She'd just begun to prepare the vegetables for supper when there was a sharp knock on the front door. Rose opened it to find a uniformed policeman smiling back at her. She invited him in, feeling a little disappointed; he appeared to be straight out of school – what would he know about bones?

Rose showed him into the kitchen and handed him the box. He took the lid off, unwrapped the paper and held it up. "You are correct – it is human, probably a young adult female. I need to make a call."

Astounded, Rose stared wide eyed at the young man, astonished by his knowledge and feeling guilty for judging him. When he ended the call he looked at Rose.

"My superior will be along shortly to take a statement."

Half an hour later, Alan pulled up outside the cottage but couldn't get his Stelvio on the drive for the two police cars blocking the entrance. Panicking he abandoned it on the road and rushed inside.

"Rose! Rose! Are you okay?" His wife was sat calmly on the sofa talking to two police officers, "What's going on?"

After identifying himself, the older of the two officers reassured Alan that it was nothing to concern himself over and that his wife wasn't a victim or a person of interest.

"Thank you for your statement, now I'm going to have to ask you to take us to the site."

This time, Rose left Nellie behind while they walked the short distance to mound. Again, Rose felt a sense of unease once she neared the area, but kept it to herself.

"What will you do now?" Alan asked, as red and white

tape was being erected to cordon off the area.

"I'm afraid we can't discuss it with you sir, we have procedures to follow. We'll be in touch if we require any more information."

Alan was unusually animated as they ate supper, "Well, I didn't think we'd be unearthing bodies in this sleepy village." But Rose was rather subdued, so he continued, "I'm sure it won't be suspicious; just one of those eco burials gone wrong."

Sighing, Rose hoped he was right, but she wasn't as optimistic. Why did she have such an apprehensive feeling about it?

30.

Life continued in an uneventful fashion and Rose was beginning to think Alan was probably right after all – an eco-burial gone wrong. That was until Tuesday morning of the following week. She was about to go out for groceries when there was another knock on the door. Rooted to the spot, she froze, certain that this was going to be bad news. It was.

"Good morning, can we come inside?"

The officer in question didn't wait for a reply but stepped into the hall. "This way, is it?" Once in the lounge he nodded. "Do take a seat."

"What is it? What have you found?"

The female officer accompanying him took over. "Is it okay if I call you Rose?" Rose nodded; her mouth now dry. "The bone that you found belongs to a young woman who was reported missing in nineteen-seventy-nine." Rose put her hand over her mouth, her worst fears now having come true.

"We'd like to ask you some more questions."

Rose nodded again, unsure as to what more she could add.

"What year were you born?"

Shocked, she looked at the young woman with mousy brown hair tumbling out of her messy bun, realising she was probably old enough to be her mother.

"Nineteen- sixty- three. Why?"

"Where were you born?"

Rose stared open mouthed at the female officer with an uneasy sensation in the pit of her stomach.

"Have you ever attended any protest meetings in the past?"

"No, I haven't! And why do you need to know about me?" Rose asked incredulously.

"So, you would have been sixteen at the time. Where were you living?"

Rose couldn't believe her ears. "Why is this relevant?"

"This is now a murder inquiry and…"

"You think I killed this poor girl?" Rose's voice had now risen an octave. "This is ridiculous!"

"We need to do some checks so we can rule you out."

Silence descended on the room and the male officer took over. "I'm sorry Rose, we don't think you did this, but we have to follow protocol to make sure your evidence fits. You did disturb the burial site."

The last comment was more than Rose was prepared to take. She stood up, squared her shoulders and faced both officers. "I did not disturb the burial site, my dog did!"

The male officer scratched his chin and lowered his voice "Yes, but what were you doing on private land...?"

"I was chasing after my dog. She'd run off!"

"There was a big sign saying it was private."

Now furious, Rose continued. "I'm sorry officer, my dog can't read. She is clever, but reading is a skill she hasn't quite mastered yet!"

Realising he wasn't getting anywhere, he stepped back, placed his hat back on and turned. "Thank you for your time. I have to ask that you don't leave the country without notifying us first."

"What is this, good cop – bad cop?" After pausing she added, "I'll show you out."

"Erm, first we'd like you to give a DNA sample..."

Rose had now had enough. "Please leave!"

Once they'd left, Rose sat down and began to shake. It was only nine-thirty, but she needed a stiff drink. Quickly pouring a tumbler full of the first bottle she came to in the cabinet, she took a large gulp and sighed. The golden liquid burned her throat and made her eyes sting, what was it. She read the bottle. Macallan Gold – Alan's favourite. Knocking the rest of the generous glass back, she sat down and sagged; she could see why. The warming liquid had found its way into her stomach, then very quickly into her blood stream. She couldn't go to the farm shop now, but she needed to talk to Alan.

"Sorry Rose, he's in a management meeting." Once again it was the voice of Peter, his assistant.

"Tell him it's urgent!"

Alan was furious when Rose told him about her visit from the police and made a call to their solicitor who in turn recommended a colleague, Mr Sykes, who would be able to advise. A short while later, he rang Rose back.

"It appears it's nothing to worry about, Love, it's routine. But Mr Sykes recommends that we make a formal complaint about the way you were treated."

Rose blew out a long breath. She felt sleepy now; the whiskey had done its job. "No Alan, don't, it's not worth the bother."

"Well, if they come back, tell them that they need to make an appointment to see you when I'm in."

Her shopping list and bag were abandoned in the kitchen. She'd have to get the groceries tomorrow; she couldn't drive now. Irritated, she clumsily snatched her bag off the work surface, spilling its contents onto the floor. Once her eyes had focused, she began to pick the items up, her car keys, a diary and a tissue along with a pen and a packet of mints. One of the small mints had fallen out of its container onto the floor. Rose bent to pick it up before Nellie found it. She was about to drop it in the bin when she paused. It wasn't a mint. Carefully she examined the small, white object. It was a tooth. But where had it come from? Horrified she dropped it back onto the kitchen surface. A tooth! Rose froze. It had dropped out of her bag – the same bag that she'd put the jawbone in to bring it home. Stepping back, she stared at the offending item as though it might come to life. What should she do? Her shoulders sagged and she sighed. Nothing. She'd do nothing. She was going to keep it. It was of no value to the police investigation; they'd already identified the body. Rose picked it up between her thumb and fore finger holding it up to the light. It was hers now. Unable to fight the after effects of the large tumbler of whiskey any longer, she made her way to their bedroom, placed the tooth on her bedside cabinet and quickly fell into a deep sleep.

A young woman popped her head out of a makeshift tent and called to a man cooking sausages over an open fire. "Flint, have you seen Sabine?"

The unkempt looking man, wearing a stained vest that had presumably been white at one time, ran his hand through his rough stubble and shrugged. "Morning Helen, sorry, haven't seen her for a couple of days."

Looking back down into his burnt pan, he continued poking a fat sausage with a stick.

Helen looked around and saw Linda drawing a bucket of water from the tank in the centre of the camp. "Have you seen Sabine?"

Linda put her bucket down and sauntered over. "Saw her the night before last. She was leaving the camp."

"Where was she going?"

"No idea." Linda paused for a moment, staring into the distance. "Didn't she say she was going home soon?"

"Oh, that's next week, her brother's getting married in Germany."

Shrugging her shoulders, Linda went back to her task then turned and waved a hand dismissively. "She's always been a party animal. She'll be back in a day or two nursing a hangover."

A low rumbling noise on the periphery of Rose's consciousness roused her from her slumber. Slowly sitting up, she rubbed her eyes and looked out of the window. It was only the bin men. Groggily, she stumbled back to bed where sleep quickly overcame her once more.

"Thank you for attending." It was Helen standing in the centre of the camp with at least eight others sitting around a fire pit. "As you know, Sabine hasn't returned,

and we don't know where she is."

A rotund woman wearing a multi-coloured, tie-dyed T-shirt and matching tiered skirt held up her hand. "Did you find any clues in her tent?"

"Nothing unusual I'm afraid. A vase of dead flowers and a wedding invitation. Her brother got married last week."

"Well – that's where she'll be, she always did like a party," another replied.

"I'd have thought she'd be back by now. Tomorrow's a big day – as you know, a major operation begins this week at the American base. Our sisters will be relying on us for support. We need to swell the numbers, disrupt as much as possible."

"Have you thought – she might already be at the base? Like you say – she wouldn't miss it for the world. She was instrumental in setting all of this up." This time it was Flint speaking, the only male member of the small satellite group who helped behind the scenes with logistics. Their work was invaluable to the efforts of the CND camp outside the American base.

"Possibly, but it's not like her to go off radar. We'll find out tomorrow I guess." Helen stretched and yawned. "Anyway, let's get some shut eye - we've got a big day ahead of us. Flint, is the van loaded with supplies?"

Flint nodded, his once chiselled face wrinkled now as he smiled. He was proud and fiercely protective of these young women, giving up so much while trying to avert a global disaster by grabbing the attention of the media – and the world. He rubbed his hand over his grey stubble, wishing he felt as optimistic as he sounded. He'd seen a couple of young men hanging around twice now, but they always disappeared into the undergrowth when spotted. He would recognise their type anywhere. Military personnel! Probably Americans. They weren't in uniform, but it was obvious to him. He should know, he'd served at the end of the war when he'd been a young man. Were they here on a spying mission or was it personal? Sighing, he ran his hand over his abdomen – he'd been proud of his physique back then, but his six-pack had long been replaced by flab. Fifty-five, where had the years gone? No, he was in no fit state to take them on anymore. 'Should he mention it to Helen?' he mused. Probably not – it would only cause her more anxiety. Hopefully, Sabine would be waiting for them outside the base tomorrow.

A pounding sensation behind Rose's eyes disrupted her dream. Where was she? Slowly, she prised one eye open, closing it again quickly, wishing she hadn't. The strong sunlight did nothing for her throbbing head. Groaning, she rolled over. Why did she feel so bad? The whiskey! What a stupid thing to do! And during the day! What had she been thinking?

Reluctantly, she left her bed and went to the kitchen for

water, her mouth as dry as the sands of the Sahara Desert. Sauntering into the dining room to her altar, she saw the German vase from the sixties that she'd bought at her first antiques fair. She thought back to the night when she'd had her first vision about Sabine. That vase had prompted it. Had it belonged to her? It was a possibility, but she'd never know. If only she could've seen the vase inside Sabine's tent! She picked it up and carried it to her bedroom, depositing the tooth inside. She then placed it on her bedside cabinet and lay back down. Could she return to her vision? There was only one way to find out.

This time, sleep was hard to come by; it was nearly midday and the alcohol haze had worn off. Continuing, she tried her best, closing her eyes, deep breathing, meditation and visualisation – but nothing worked. Frustrated, she sat up and put her aching head in her hands and cried. Once her sobs had subsided, she stood and stared out of the window.

"Why me?" she shouted, holding her hands up to the ceiling. "Why is all of this weird stuff happening to me?"

But her question remained unanswered. Chastising herself, Rose made a smoked salmon and cream cheese sandwich and sat on the patio with Nellie. She needed to pull herself together, she needed to solve all of these mysteries that had somehow presented themselves to her. But how? Now was not the time to wallow in self-pity. Now was the time to act! Jumping up, she went inside and grabbed her notebook. It was time to prioritise! Which mystery was the most important to solve? She already knew the answer. This one. Sabine. She had to discover how and why Sabine had been murdered. But she needed help. Her first, though, was Alan. They'd always supported each other through difficult times like family bereavements – but this was different. His opinion was 'leave it to the police, it's their job not yours – don't get involved.' But she was already involved – she'd discovered the body and was now a potential suspect, even though she'd been a child at the time and had lived miles away. It was a ridiculous situation.

Turning to a clean page she wrote the mysteries down in a neat list –

1 Joseph and Ester during the war.

2 Sabine.

3 William, Anne and Lavinia.

4 John in Canada.

Sighing, she put her book down. Four mysteries, there were only four mysteries. She picked her pen back up and turned another page and wrote the heading SABINE, underlining it several times. Quickly, she scribbled down every detail that she knew about the case from her visions. It wasn't much to go on, but she was feeling better now, stronger. Somehow, she knew that this challenge had been sent to her for a reason and she had to solve it. She would solve it! But where should she begin? Rose's head snapped up – it was the doorbell. The last thing she needed today was another visit from the police. It was no good informing them about her visions – they'd never take her seriously! Nervously, she walked down the hall and held her breath before opening the door, her speech already prepared.

"You need to make an app…"

"Hi Rose, I couldn't stop thinking about you. Are you okay?"

Rose sagged then threw her arms around Freya, her strength now gone, and began to cry once more.

Freya made Rose a cup of chamomile tea and held her hand while she listened as Rose poured out her heart, telling her about the visit from the police.

"I'm so glad that you've told me – I knew something was wrong."

"Why me Freya?"

Freya squeezed her hand. "Because you have the gift Rose."

Rose's brow furrowed. "But why now – I'm nearly sixty?"

THE WITCH'S CHAIR

"It's the cottage Rose – and the antiques. They are oozing history and energy and you're picking up on it." Rose frowned so Freya continued. "You've always been too busy Rose, running after your family - living in modern houses in busy towns. Your existence has changed so much. A slower pace of life in an old building submerged deep in the countryside. There's no rumbling traffic and fewer distractions. You're no longer a taxi service for your daughters. You've become much more aware of the seasons and the cycles of the moon. You're a witch Rose, a wise woman. We both are, that's why we found each other. And together we can solve these mysteries – but we'll need Shona's help too."

Rose's eyes widened. "No more witchcraft in my house! I'm not risking Shona setting my house on fire again!"

Smiling Freya sat back. "Agreed, we'll work outside." Freya turned and looked out of the window, "How are you getting on with your internet search about William, Anne and Lavinia?"

"To be honest – I've given up. The trail went cold – I seemed to hit a dead end."

Freya tried not to show her frustration. She was desperate to find out what Anne needed to tell her. "Never mind," she sighed, "I think this murder enquiry takes priority, don't you?"

Nodding, Rose agreed. "But where do we start?"

"The scene of the crime. Let's go back to where you found the body and begin there."

31.

"Count me in – I'll meet you there. Tell Rose to bring the tooth and Nellie." Shona ended the call and smiled; this was her forte. She'd been involved in two cold cases previously when she'd lived in the city. That was before she'd relocated to the countryside with her husband after her first child was born, Maisy, a precious daughter, and it had been liberating – her perception had sharpened considerably. She was ready for the challenge.

"Have you got it?" Freya asked, leaning her bicycle against a tree.

Nodding, Rose held up the tooth between her thumb and finger, then looked back down the lane to see Shona striding towards them with a rucksack strapped to her back. "I do hope she doesn't intend to start a fire!"

"Morning ladies, give me a moment." Kneeling down, Shona emptied her bag onto the woodland floor.

"What have you brought?" Rose asked, trying to hide her anxiety.

"Just the essentials – don't want to draw attention to ourselves. Now let me have a look around."

The small mound and surrounding area that had

previously been covered in nettles now looked like a war zone – it reminded Rose of her lawn and drive after Jim had dug the hole for her pond. She shook her head, trying to rid herself of the memory – it seemed like a lifetime ago and she needed to concentrate.

Shona took the top off a small bottle and ingested a few drops of a tincture that she'd prepared earlier. Rose didn't ask what it was, but she felt sure it would taste vile.

Holding the bottle out she passed it to Freya, who followed suit then gave it to Rose. She was right, it smelled like a wet compost heap.

"Just do it!" Shona ordered.

Rose held her breath, placed three drops onto her tongue and quickly swallowed. It was vile.

"Good, now give me the tooth."

Complying, Rose passed it to Shona and watched as she began her work. First, she held it up to the light to examine it carefully then she placed it in her right hand and began to walk clockwise around the excavated area. Freya followed her, and Rose tagged on behind. Shona began to chant quietly before suddenly stopping. Her head snapped up. "Can you feel anything?"

Concentrating, Rose realised that she couldn't; the cold eerie feeling had gone.

"No. It's gone. The feeling has gone, and Nellie isn't interested either," Rose answered. "What now?"

"She wasn't murdered on this spot; it was just a convenient burial site." Shona looked around. "Let's split up. Freya, you go north, I'll take west. Rose, you cover south, and let Nellie off her lead."

Each of the three women set off on different bearings, Rose slowly walking in the direction she was given, wondering why Shona had left east out of the equation. Brambles scratched her legs, and she clambered over fallen logs with Nellie scampering on eagerly. After a while Nellie stopped abruptly, put her head in the air and turned sharp right. Instinctively, Rose followed her hoping that she wouldn't get a reprimand from Shona, but she couldn't leave Nellie. A short while later, she popped out into a grassy clearing surrounded by trees and dense undergrowth. Nellie sat down and whimpered. Rose sat quietly by her side, glad that she was alone. A cold shiver ran up her spine and she froze. Soon, a strange smell permeated her nostrils – it wasn't pleasant. Rose couldn't place it, a cross between disinfectant and tom cat wee. Colours began to wheel around behind her eyelids, psychedelic colours. Drugs. It was cannabis. That's what she could smell. Was this the spot? Nellie thought so. Looking around, she sighed wishing that she hadn't given the tooth to Shona. Would she be able to have a vision without it? It was worth a try, after all – she'd taken some of Shona's wonder juice. Rose reached out and scraped up a fist full of earth in her right hand then stood and walked around the edge of the small clearing in a clockwise direction chanting 'Right to receive.' Nellie followed her then they both perched on a nearby fallen log. Rose rolled her shoulders to release the tension, closed her eyes and took three deep breaths. She felt sure this was the very spot – and she was right.

"You weren't meant to fucking kill her Hank! Just rough her up a little – that was the brief. Scare the shit out of them."

Hank knelt beside the limp body of a young woman, her skirt hitched up around her waist. He ran his hands through his cropped black hair and began to panic then looked back to his buddy. "Shit! I, I, didn't do anything that would've killed her – surely!" He stood up and paced around the edge of the clearing muttering to himself, "Fuck! Now what?"

"Tidy her up. Did you use a condom?" It was Phil, the senior of the two men barking orders, his brain now gone into authoritarian mode. It was work. He was on an assignment, and assignments could go wrong. It was a risk they understood only too well, but the powers that be wouldn't be impressed. He stood up to his full height, six foot two inches, and wiped his sweaty palms down his black T shirt, while his mind whirred. He was now back in Vietnam. He'd seen enough atrocities to last a lifetime; this was nothing by comparison. The CIA wanted rid of them, now there was one less. Mission

accomplished. His head snapped up; decision made. "Drag her under those bushes behind you. We'll come back tomorrow night with shovels. Job done. No one will be any the wiser."

Rose was in a crumpled pile, sobbing in the clearing, when her friends found her. Freya rushed to her side and enveloped her in a hug.

"What is it Rose? Have you had a vision?"

When her sobs eventually subsided, Shona pressed a hip flask containing brandy to her lips then they both listened without interruption while Rose recounted her story.

"Right, can you walk now?" Shona asked, packing her tools of the trade back into her bag.

Nodding, Rose patted her sore eyes with a tissue. "What should we do?"

"Go to the police of course."

Rose stared at Shona. "Are you mad? They'll just think I'm certifiable!"

"No, they won't – trust me. I have a contact in the city, Amelia, a consultant for the criminal physiology department. She's quite open to using the services of mediums. I've worked with them before. She'll want to talk to you."

"Mm, I'm not so sure…"

Freya helped Rose to her feet. "Come on, let's get you home. Shona will contact Amelia and we'll all go together."

Shona was right, Amelia was very interested and dismissed Rose's concerns, "Don't worry about your local police, we'll take over now. They won't bother you again." Amelia handed the three women a card each with various contact numbers. "If anything else comes to you, let me know, no matter how trivial it may seem."

"Will you be able to find the perpetrators?" Rose asked as they were shown out of the building.

"We'll do our best, but it's not that simple when other agencies are involved. Thank you for coming. I'll be in touch."

When Rose returned home, she sagged with relief. She felt so sorry for Sabine but glad she'd been able to help. It was no longer her problem.

Alan arrived home from work later that day and gave Rose a customary peck on the cheek. "You look a little flushed, Love. Have you had a good day?"

Rose smiled and nodded. If only you knew, she thought to herself, while keeping her lips sealed.

It was over a week before the three women met again,

this time at Shona's.

"Have you heard from Amelia?" Rose asked hopefully.

"Yes, that's why I've asked you over, well, that and a catch up."

Rose looked at Shona's face hoping it was good news. It wasn't.

"She's hit a brick wall."

"How? Why?" Rose questioned impatiently.

"Official secrets act – and all of that stuff."

Incredulously, Rose let her frustrations rip. "That's – that's, not fair! Surely, when there's a murder involved, they can give out information!"

"Apparently not – diplomatic immunity. It sucks, I know. I'm sorry Rose. You can't win them all."

Rose sagged in her chair and dropped her head into her hands. "What now?"

"We carry on Rose." It was Freya, as always comforting her friend.

Shona tried to interject some hope. "It will be kept on record and after a set period of time Amelia's team will try again, but she's not optimistic I'm afraid. When the Americans want something in return, they sometimes trade secrets, but this case is no biggie to all concerned."

Again, Rose was furious. "It's a 'biggie' to Sabine and her family. And to me!"

Freya took Rose's hand. "I know, and I'm sorry, but at least her family have closure. They have her body and can now lay her to rest."

The three women sat in contemplative silence for a while then Rose jumped up. "I think we should hold a small ritual; nothing elaborate – and no fires. Perhaps we could plant a tree on the site and some wildflowers?"

"Yes, that's a lovely idea."

Rose felt a little lighter. "No time like the present. Let's go to the nursery where I got my fruit trees and chose something, it's not far."

The next day they went back to Sabine's burial site and held a short service then planted a young rowan tree to mark the spot. Rose placed the tooth in the bottom of the hole before scooping the earth back. Next, Rose led them to the murder site where they planted a mixture of spring flowering bulbs. It was the closure that Rose needed.

32.

The spiritual meetings began again in September, when the children had returned to school, after a long dry summer. Shona had decided that it was time for Rose to host her first meeting, but Rose wasn't too sure.

"What if William or Anne make an appearance? What will the others think?"

Shona was perplexed. "We frequently hold meetings at mine, and nothing happens."

Rose snapped back. "That's because you live in a new build! You frightened them away from Freya's house."

Freya kept quiet; she was desperate to communicate with William or Anne again – they had news for her. Unfinished business. She didn't want to upset Rose, but this was important to her.

"Mm." Shona thought for a minute. Perhaps Rose was right. "Okay, let's do it in the garden. We'll keep it light, a short blessing, then get everyone to tell us about their summer adventures."

Rose still wasn't convinced, but she reluctantly agreed. It sounded more like the first day back at primary school to her, but she'd go along with it. She now knew that the Wednesday meetings weren't really for her anymore. Yes, she'd met Shona and Freya and they'd formed a strong bond. She'd host this one meeting but it would be her last.

Freya arrived early and helped Rose to arrange the chairs in the front garden around the pond. It wasn't as magical as Alison's garden, but it was hers and she loved it. Her confidence was growing alongside her newfound ability, and she was beginning to accept that she really was a witch. She knew that she'd have to confess to Alan soon but dreaded the thought. He was very set in his ways and obsessed with his cars; little else seemed to be of importance to him. He'd probably think she'd lost the plot. Would this send him running into the arms of his mistress? Possibly, but that was something else she needed to face too. They couldn't continue living with deception. If the worst came to the worst then they would have to come to a mutual agreement. Yes, it was time to slay the dragon.

"There are only six garden chairs. Is it okay if I fetch a couple from inside?"

Rose was distracted, arranging cushions and throws to make her guests more comfortable, when Freya came back with more chairs. It wasn't until several of the others had arrived that she noticed Freya had brought the old rocking chair out. Rose stared at Freya and then back at the chair, but Freya pretended not to notice. She was desperate to find out what William and Anne had to tell her and knew this might be an opportunity. They'd joined a 'witch's group – what did they expect?

Freya immediately sat in the old rocking chair, making sure no one else got the seat. As far as she was concerned, it was the seat of power and she was going to occupy it.

Suddenly, Rose realised what Freya was up to and began to worry; she needed to take control. It was her meeting. She was the host and couldn't allow the session to get out of hand. She felt a little hurt that Freya was doing this, but knew she needed to 'man up'. Freya was strong and Rose was going to show her that she could be too. So, she squared her shoulders and looked at her friend.

"Freya, could you bring the cakes out please?"

"Ooh, yummy, what have you made?" one of the women asked.

Freya considered her options while looking from one face to another, but all eyes were on her; she'd got no choice. She picked her bag up off the floor and placed it on her seat hoping that would be enough to deter anyone else from claiming it and did as she was asked. When she returned her bag was placed on a table and Rose was sitting in the rocking chair. Shona watched on with amusement, realising what was at play between the two women. She hadn't expected Rose to be so bold, but was thrilled to see her gaining confidence at long last.

"Over to you Rose, it's your meeting."

Shock spread across Rose's face. What was she supposed to say? Eventually, after a long pause, she found her inner strength.

"Good morning, ladies, welcome back." She looked over to Shona for reassurance, then found her voice. "Thank you for coming. Today, I'd like to celebrate the beginning of the harvest." Rose had no idea where any of this was coming from, but carried on with her sermon. "If you look around us you can see the bountiful fruits that mother nature has provided." Rose pointed to her fruit trees in her small meadow; although still small they were festooned with apples and pears. Thinking that this truly was like being back at primary school for the harvest festival, she wondered whether she should burst into song. 'We plough the fields and scatter the good seed on the land' immediately came to mind but she dismissed the thought and invited the group to go and help themselves to a piece of fruit. When they'd returned, biting into their juicy bounty, Rose invited them all to tell the group about their adventures over the summer holiday. They were eager participants and Alison volunteered to go first.

She began recounting her three-week holiday in the south of France, but unfortunately Rose was struggling to listen; William had arrived.

"Go away!" Rose hissed.

"Pardon?" Alison asked, with a look of concern.

Freya jumped up, she immediately knew what was happening. "It's just a pesky wasp. Rose is allergic to stings."

Shona took over with a twinkle in her eye, this was going to be fun. "Thank you, Alison, that sounds wonderful. Who wants to go next?"

"Not now!" Rose blurted out, shocking the group.

"Are you okay Rose?" one of the wide-eyed women asked.

"Yes, erm, sorry, unwelcome visitors."

Freya was quick to respond. "Would you like to swap seats Rose? I'm not usually troubled by wasps."

Shona watched on in fascination while her two friends continued with their battle, the other members now looking slightly confused on the periphery. Rose glared at Freya. Now was not the time, but Freya had decided it was. Rose was adamant that William wasn't going to spoil the meeting, but it seemed that William too had other ideas. He really must have something important to say.

"Enough!" Rose stood up and squeezed her eyes tight shut. She somehow needed to end this meeting. "I'm so sorry ladies, I've just been stung by an uninvited visitor; I need to get my medication. Thank you for coming."

Shona jumped up and took over her role as leader, showing the confused women out onto the drive. "So sorry, it's a terrible time of year for wasps."

When she returned, Freya was in the rocking chair looking disappointed. "He's gone – you've frightened him away!"

Trying not to laugh, Shona managed a straight face. "Freya, that wasn't very fair of you."

Looking a little guilty and feeling like a naughty schoolgirl, Freya apologised. "I'm sorry Rose – what did he want?"

"So you should be, you ruined the meeting!"

"I know, but I need to know what he wants."

Feeling a little sorry for her friend, Rose sighed, "I don't know Freya. I was trying to shoo him away. He kept repeating one word."

Now excited, Freya shouted, "What?"

"Family," Rose replied, "he kept saying family."

"Whose family?"

"I'm sorry Freya, I don't know anymore."

Shona interrupted. "I think we need to get to the bottom of this."

"Yes, it's on my list, as well as Esther and Joseph. How did their clock end up here? And the candlesticks?"

"I thought we'd solved the candlestick mystery. They came over on a boat."

Rose cocked her head to one side. "Yes, but how did they end up at the antiques fair?"

Shona looked between her two friends. Colleagues. They were now a team and she felt they could unpick some of the mysteries together. "You can't solve everything Rose, there are far more questions than answers. And more mysteries will present themselves to us. We'll have to work together and prioritise."

Freya was the first to answer. "Well, I vote for William and Anne!"

Exhausted after this morning's performance, Rose sagged. She felt sure William and Anne weren't going anywhere in a hurry. She now accepted that they kind of lived here - caught between time and the sturdy walls of the old cottage. She almost liked it, but wasn't sure that Alan would be as enthusiastic about their house guests as she was. But the clock was an entirely separate matter – she hadn't had any visions about the clock for a long time. Yes, the clock had to be her priority. Of course, she'd help Freya – they were a team, but there was nothing to stop her working on the clock mystery herself.

Shona broke into her thoughts. "When is Alan away again for one of his motor sport things?"

"Erm, a week on Friday. Why?"

"Perfect. We'll meet here at dusk then and try again to communicate with them."

33.

Glad that her two friends had now gone, Rose went into the lounge with a cup of tea and wilted into a comfy chair. Exhaustion soon took over; her eyelids were heavy and the last thing she remembered was Edward striking twelve noon.

A large framed woman in a pale blue tunic entered the room with a frail looking woman clutching her arm. "What did you say Frieda?"

Frieda didn't stop for air, she kept on with her quiet, incomprehensible babble.

"Frieda," the woman continued, "speak to me in English – you know we don't understand German."

But Frieda wasn't listening. She allowed the carer to lower her fragile body into a sturdy, wing-backed chair, and stared into space with a glazed expression. She didn't like it here, no one understood her, and where was Gunther, her precious son? Why didn't he visit anymore?

"Gunther," a soft whisper left her lips.

"He's not here Frieda, he lives in America now." The features of the carer softened in pity. Poor Freida, she

thought - all alone.

"Home," another silent plea from the heart, barely perceptible, followed on.

"This is your home now Frieda. Your house is being sold so you can stay here with your new friends."

The carer smiled and stood back so that Frieda could see the other residents sitting out their days, hunched around the impersonal space as though they were waiting for something – or someone. Freida sighed; if this was her lot then she'd have to retreat even further into her head. She found that she was revisiting her childhood more frequently now, trying to make sense of it; a time that previously she'd shut into a box and never spoken about. Not even her dear Gunther knew the real truth, the atrocities that she'd witnessed. No, she'd never spoken of it – but now it was all she had. Her hand trembled and she startled when she heard a loud bang, someone dropping a walking stick, but to Frieda it was the sound of approaching gunfire. Sagging even further into the uncomfortable chair, her head drooped forward and she gasped.

Her eyes were gritty, and her mouth parched. Pain radiated from the infected blister on the back of her left heel. The soft, leather shoes that she'd been wearing were now in tatters – no longer a barrier to the dust and pebbles that found their way in, only to aggravate her misery. But she couldn't stop. Her mother kept urging her on.

"Not much further to go now, Liebling, then we'll rest. The sun will be coming up soon and we must reach the shelter of the forest."

Frieda whimpered, "Papa." More than anything she wanted her dear Papa. Surely, he would help them.

Esther cradled her small daughter and tried to hide the flash of pain that seared through her soul. "Papa had to go away, but we'll soon be able to rest, and eat."

Frieda thought back to the warm apple and cinnamon strudel that her Oma used to make, her favourite. Her mouth began to water.

Suddenly, she felt a hand a on her bony shoulder.

"Here's a tissue Frieda, and a cup of tea."

Frieda's eyes focused for a moment. Her body sagged even further. She was back in reality, a living hell. Was it any better than her childhood memories?

Ding-dong. Rose jumped out of her chair, knocking the now cold cup of tea off the small side table. The trill noise repeated itself. It was the doorbell. By the time that she'd pulled herself together the caller had gone, and an Amazon parcel was placed on the doorstep.

Frustrated, Rose mopped up the spilt tea then stared about the room, her eyes landing on the clock. Edward. If only he could talk. She carefully picked the old timepiece up and re-examined it hoping to find something new, but she didn't. All she knew was that it had been produced in Berlin in nineteen-ten by Joseph's father. How had it found its way to England? Sighing, Rose placed Edward back on the mantle shelf. She had to assume that Esther and Frieda had thankfully been successful in their journey to escape from the Nazis.

Frustration gnawed away at her insides; how could she find out? If only she'd taken more time to talk to the man that had sold her the clock. Her mind drifted back to that day, more than a year ago now. Her strongest memory of the event was the thunderstorm which encouraged them to seek shelter under the trader's awning. Looking back, she could now see that the storm probably hadn't been a coincidence either; it had been fate. Her friends agreed that she was meant to obtain these objects for a reason, and Rose was beginning to think they were correct. Amy had been with her that day. Rose pondered, "I wonder if she can remember anything else." She looked back at Edward. It was lunchtime; she could text Amy at lunchtime without disturbing her too much.

I'd like to get in touch with the trader we bought the clock from. I know you took lots of photos – did you by any chance get a picture of his motorhome? Wondering if it had an email or phone contacts on the side. Xx

She knew it was a long shot, but it was worth a try.

It was later that evening when she got her reply. It was a photograph of Rose standing under the awning holding Edward in her hands, and on the side of the motorhome was a name and number.

Amazing! Thank you darling. Xx

Rose was over the moon and jumped up from her chair. "Yes! Yes! Yes!"

Alan stared at his wife open mouthed. "What? Have we won the lottery?"

"No, you know I don't do the lottery," she snapped back, then composed herself and explained, offering only the bare minimum. "I've been wanting to get in touch with a trader from the antique fair and Amy has his details."

Alan shrugged, not taking much interest, it was only later that night when his bladder had woken him that he wondered if she had developed an interest in antiques because of another man.

As soon as Alan had left for work the following morning, she rang the number, bursting with anticipation.

"Good morning, you may not remember, but last summer I bought an Edwardian clock from you in the middle of a thunderstorm."

As if on cue Edward struck eight-thirty and Rose beamed.

"Erm, vaguely. How can I help?"

"I'm fascinated to find out its history, how it ended up in North Yorkshire, when it was made in Germany."

"That's easy – the war. A fair few German paintings and antiques found their way to the UK."

"Yes, but how did you come across it?"

"House clearance – that's what I do."

"Oh, I see. Do you remember anything about the occupants of the house?"

A short pause followed. "I do so many – I'd have to look at my books."

"That's very kind of you, can I ring you back?"

"Give me an hour."

Then the line went dead. A long hour passed; she redialled the number, but it went to voicemail. Another hour passed and she tried again with no luck. Pacing the room Rose was unable to put her mind to anything else. She could wait no longer.

"Hello, sorry to bother you again..."

"Ah, got caught up with a client."

"Did you find anything?"

"Yes, it belonged to an elderly lady who was going into care."

A smile cracked Rose's face in half. "Amazing, where did she live, what was she called?" Silence followed. "Do you have her details?"

"Erm, unfortunately, I can't give details out."

Rose's euphoria was quickly dashed. "Oh, can't you tell me anything?"

"Sorry. I didn't deal with the old lady; I only spoke to her son in America. He was going to put the house on the market."

"Where was the house? Just the name of a town or a village would help."

An audible sigh came down the phone line, "It was a bungalow in Thorby, near Ripon. Very run down. Probably bought by a developer now."

Excitement bubbled back up from deep within. "Thank you, thank you so much!"

It wasn't much to go on, but it was a start, and it matched the details in the vision – an elderly lady going into care with a son in America. Yes. It had to be the same lady. But was it Frieda, or her sibling? Thorby, near Ripon, it wasn't that far away. Should she jump in her car and go?

"No," she said out loud, "I'll search the internet first."

Within minutes she was looking on Rightmove. Once she'd set her parameters and included 'sold subject to contract' the number of options had whittled down to three. Two of them were sold and the other said 'unexpectedly back on the market' and 'in need of modernisation'. Blinking, Rose couldn't believe her luck. Was this the one? It matched the criteria, an old, dilapidated bungalow in Thorby. She felt sure it was. Rose scrolled through the images in front of her eyes, most of them were photos of the exterior of the property and the large gardens, which were a tangled mess and in need of attention. Without thinking she picked up her phone.

"Yes, good morning. I'd like to view the old bungalow you have for sale in Thorby please."

"It only came back on the market at the weekend; a developer had put an offer in but couldn't get planning permission."

"Can I come today?"

"We're a bit short staffed today, I'm sorry..."

"Oh! But I don't need to be accompanied; can't I collect the key? I'll be fine by myself."

"Sorry, it's not very safe, there's a hole in the kitchen

area where a slow leak has rotted the floorboards away. To be honest it needs gutting back to a shell – or pulling down."

Feeling the opportunity slipping away Rose tried again. "Could you give me the address and I'll go and view it from the outside – to be honest, it was the gardens I was most interested in."

"Yes, I can do that, but be careful, its rather overgrown. Apparently, it was once a smallholding, the vendors used to keep hens and goats and grow their own vegetables – but that was a long time ago."

Without another thought, Rose bundled Nellie into her small car, set her satnav, and drove to Thorby.

It was only a half-hour drive and Rose soon arrived onto a small country lane where her satnav informed her that she had reached her destination. There were no properties in sight. She was in the middle of nowhere. Twisting around in her seat, she scanned the area, wondering what to do. Should she ring the estate agent back? A quick glance at her phone revealed that she had no signal. Great. Instinctively, she continued down the narrow road until a loud yap from Nellie made her stop. Looking around once more, she noticed an entrance on her left, concealed by a hedge that would've been a worthy challenge for the prince on his mission to find Sleeping Beauty. Was this the place? Nellie seemed to think so. With caution, she held her breath and shoehorned her car through the gap to find the for-sale sign propped against what was left of a gate. A prickling sensation travelled down the length of her spine and Nellie yapped again. This had to be the one.

The once gravelled drive, winding into the distance, was pocked with craters and covered in vegetation. Rose followed its outline the best she could round a sharp bend then suddenly bust out through a tangle of bushes into bright sunlight. It was blinding; one of those rare, late, summer days where thin, wispy clouds meandered across a cobalt blue sky. Once her eyes had acclimatised to the brightness, she gasped. Before her sat an imposing detached bungalow of magnificent proportions. Abandoning her car, she released Nellie and stood in wonder. Clearly, the façade had once been majestic, way superior to her beloved cottage. She was spellbound. Her eyes flitted from the gabled roofs to the impressive chimney then down to the columns supporting the front porch. In its heyday it would have been magnificent, but to Rose's eyes it still was.

"Wow!" She was speechless.

But her euphoria quickly turned to anger. How could anyone be allowed to demolish this amazing building. Surely it should be listed. Her mind wandered back to her earlier conversation with the estate agent – 'the property developer couldn't get planning permission'. Perhaps there was hope for it after all. Relaxing a little, she navigated a path through the nettles and thistles up to the front door. The details were exquisite, from the intricate carvings on the wood to the now dulled brass doorknocker. It was splendid. Thoughts of the interior beckoned; she felt sure it would have an amazing inglenook fireplace. Stepping round the bindweed clinging to the oak columns, she peered through a window sectioned into small squares of glass set in lead. Some of the panes higher up were coloured to form a pattern. To her disappointment, she couldn't see much; years of grime were stuck to their surface. Wiping her hand across one small pane of glass, she stopped suddenly. The glass wobbled, worked loose by the passage of time and subsequent neglect. Afraid to cause any damage, she stepped back before deciding to try a window nearer the corner. That was no better. Never mind, she'd found the property. Perhaps she'd stumble across more clues in the grounds.

Calling Nellie to her side, Rose turned down the side of the property where she came across a greenhouse and a potting shed. Treading carefully, she picked Nellie up when they encountered shards of glass from the greenhouse now scattered on the floor. The potting shed looked more promising though. A rusty bolt was the first obstacle, but with perseverance it eventually yielded, leaving Rose peering inside the gloomy space. Tentatively stepping inside, her eyes darted around its interior. Scampering sounds caught Nellie's attention, rodents no doubt. An old, discarded gardening glove with several missing fingertips confirmed Rose's suspicions. Mice. Rose picked it up and examined it closely; the pink floral pattern was now dulled with age and use. Had it belonged to Frieda? Almost certainly.

In the far corner, next to a sturdy bench, was a navy-blue raincoat hung on a rusty nail. Reaching over, she took it down. It was petite, probably a size eight. She desperately wanted to try it on but knew she wouldn't be able to fit into the garment. Her hands instinctively made their way to the patch pocket on the side of the coat. Hoping not to come across too many minibeasts, she closed her eyes and delved within. Inside, she could feel a small pencil and a scrap of paper. Retrieving the two objects, she stared wide eyed. There was writing on the paper. It was a list, but it wasn't in English. It was written in a foreign language. Could it be German? It certainly looked like it. It took Rose a little while as she tried hard to remember back to her German lessons from her school days. She was indeed at the correct address. It appeared to be a list of vegetables. With growing excitement, she slowly translated them. Carrots, peas, lettuce, tomatoes and potatoes. Was it a shopping list? Were these the seeds that Frieda was planting? She needed to see more. Much more.

Rose was about to step back outside into the sunshine when a bizarre sensation overcame her; her body sagged, feeling as though her head and limbs were made out of lead. Now unsteady on her feet, she lowered herself onto a wobbly buffet, placing her head in her hands.

It was Frieda again, but this time she was sitting on a small suitcase looking forlorn on what appeared to be the deck of a large boat. She was wearing a bottle green coat with her name pinned onto her chest.

"Come along children, move closer together so we can fit everyone on board."

"Where are we going?" a young boy wailed.

"England, where you'll all be safe."

A tall slim woman with a clipboard smiled and turned to a crew member. "Thank you, that's all of the orphans on board. When do we sail?"

The crew member took off his hat and bowed his head. "About an hour left now." He looked across the deck to the hundred or so children of varying ages when his gaze stopped at Frieda. "That little girl's crying."

"Yes, it's a sorry tale. She made it all the way through France with her pregnant mother but three days ago she suffered a premature birth; she was so weak that both the mother and the baby didn't survive. It was a little boy, so tiny – the poor thing didn't stand a chance."

Another sound distracted Rose; she lifted her head to find a brown hen entering the potting shed. Rubbing her eyes, she stared at the feathery creature and it stared back at her. Nellie looked from the hen back to Rose, waiting for a signal. Was it a friend or a foe?

Rose held out her hand. "Hello, where did you come from?"

The hen turned around, hopped out of the shed, and scurried off into the tangled garden. Were these Frieda's hens? Had they been abandoned? How could she find out? Now on a mission, she turned to march back to her car but another bizarre sensation rippled through her body. Smiling, she climbed back into the shed and retrieved Frieda's pencil, her shopping list and the nibbled glove. No one would miss them.

It was only when she'd got back into her car that her mind wandered back to her vision. Only Frieda had made it out safely. She'd been orphaned. What a tragic beginning to poor Frieda's life.

34.

Once back home, Rose rang the estate agent and told them about the hen.

"Oh, I didn't know there was any livestock left; it's been empty for a while. I'll contact the son in America."

It wasn't until the next day that Rose got her answer. The son had tried to catch the remaining hens, there were three of them, but, being free range, he hadn't managed to get them all.

"Can I have them?"

"I honestly don't know what to say. We've never come across this situation before."

"If you give me the son's contact details, I can ask him myself."

"I can't do that, but I could give him your details if you like – we use emails because of the time difference."

Rose beamed; the thought of actually communicating with Gunther blew her mind away.

Trying to go about her everyday chores was difficult for Rose. It had been four days now; perhaps Gunther didn't want her to have the hens after all, but how would they survive?

She'd asked Alan the same question when he'd commented about her lack of concentration the night before. "You always seem to be in a daydream lately – is something troubling you?"

She'd told him that she'd managed to track down the son of the previous owner of the clock and that she'd been interested in the story so went along to see the house that it had come from. He hadn't been too interested.

"Plenty of insects for them to eat – it's their natural diet." He then went on to remind her that he'd be away at the weekend, Wales this time apparently.

When she checked the following morning, she'd got a message from Gunther.

Hello, pleased to make your acquaintance. If you can catch the hens – they're yours. I tried when I was there in the spring when mother had her fall. Don't know if they still lay; they must be getting on in years.

Regards

Gunther Robinson.

Rose was thrilled and did a little happy dance. Yes, she could have Frieda's three remaining hens.

"Frieda Robinson," she let the name roll off her tongue. She'd married an English man and had a son, but had she been happy? 'Did she have any other children?'

Rose wondered. 'And had she ever recovered from her traumatic childhood?' Rose longed to find out, but for now she was content with the hens – and the mouse-eaten glove, shopping list and pencil. Smiling to herself, she thought about the items; the glove was in the garden shed but the list and pencil were in her bedside cabinet. She might be able to use them in future to learn more about Frieda. Was Alan right? Was she in a daydream most of the time? She pondered this question for a while and decided she probably was a little distracted; so much had been going on recently, especially with the Sabine murder enquiry. But that had come to an end and, of course, Alan didn't know the half of it. She knew that she had to tell him at some point that she was an actual witch, but she doubted that he'd take her seriously. She sighed, imagining the conversation. No, for now she decided to wait until she'd solved the William and Anne mystery; that had to be her next priority, after the hens of course. Eagerly, she responded to Gunther's email. What should she say? She couldn't very well ask him directly about his mother's life experiences. No, she'd keep it simple.

Thank you for contacting me. I bought an old clock from an antique fair last summer and I managed to follow the trail back to your mother's property; that's where I stumbled upon the hens. I'll try and catch them and relocate them to my garden. I'll keep you posted on their progress.

Regards

Rose.

Her next task was to research the requirements of hens. They would need somewhere secure at night, as Frank the fox visited regularly. Where were they roosting now, she mused? That was her next search, which shocked her. Apparently, they roosted in trees if their wings weren't clipped. Looking out of the window, Rose gazed at the spreading elm tree, overhanging the garage at the bottom of the back garden. It was a stunning tree; in fact, it was deemed so unusual by the local council to have escaped the ravages of Dutch elm disease that it had been awarded a tree preservation order. But now, Rose noticed, its leaves were beginning to take on the hues of late summer and would soon be turning russet. The earth was parched; it had been a while since the last rains. Her continued research suggested a small enclosure was indeed required for night-time, but during the day the hens would be safe in an enclosed garden. All she had to do was purchase a readymade hen hut; they were even available on Amazon. Oh, and persuade Alan – though, perhaps he wouldn't even notice. The first task was taken care of, the hen hut would arrive tomorrow, but first she had to catch them.

Freya was fascinated when Rose rang her. "Ooh yes, I'll help you. When do you want to go?"

"I can't go tomorrow; I've got a hen hut to build. Apparently, it's a flat pack, but it stipulates that it's easy to assemble."

"Text me when it arrives. I'll come and help you."

The hen hut had arrived by ten-thirty and Freya followed soon after. The two women persevered until the structure was erected between the garage and the workshop on a patch of lawn that was more moss than grass. It was a shady area that she felt sure the hens would like. A sizeable, shallow trough filled with water along with a bowl of grain and grit were added. Freya put the finishing touches to the ensemble and stuffed the coop with fresh hay. The two women stood back to admire their work. It was perfect. Now for the hens — that might not be as easy.

"I'll be here at nine in the morning with my cat carrier. It might be a squeeze, but we'll get them in."

At ten-fifteen Rose drove her car as near as possible to the potting shed, carefully avoiding the broken glass. The two women got out and stared at each other.

"Wow Rose! This is amazing!"

Nodding in agreement, Rose looked about her, noticing things she hadn't seen on her first visit, a garden pond covered in duckweed, a swing suspended beneath a sycamore tree, a wrought iron table and chairs encrusted with rust. There was so much to take in. How she wished she could have seen it in its prime.

Just as Rose was about to open the potting shed door, she heard a rustle in the bushes behind her.

"Have you got the bird seed?"

Freya nodded, producing a bag from her trouser pocket. "Here chuck, chuck, chuck."

She began to scatter seed on the ground and, as if by magic, a hen appeared. Rose took a handful of seed and bent down. Another hen appeared and both began to peck at the food. "Aww, they're hungry. There should be another one."

"It might not be here anymore…"

Determined to leave with all three hens, Rose crouched down and searched the undergrowth. "Here Freya, its hiding under here. Look!"

The two women scattered a small amount of seed under the bush, stepped back and held their breath, as slowly, the hen moved forward then stooped to gobble it up. Over the next hour, they gradually enticed the timid hen out into the open with its comrades. The bolder two hens were easy to coax into the cat carrier but the third one wasn't as confident. It took Rose and Freya all morning to eventually catch all three hens.

"What are you going to call them?" Freya asked on the drive home.

"I hadn't given that any thought – they might already

have names."

"You could ask Gunther if he knows. Send him another email."

Before long, the three new arrivals were checking out their new home. Rose took a photograph and emailed it to Gunther.

As you can see, they're safe in their new home. Do they have names?

After tea that night, Alan went outside to his garage. He smiled when he saw the hen hut; he wasn't in the least surprised. 'What would his wife do next?' he mused.

Again, the following morning, there was another response from America.

Glad they're safe and well. I'll tell Mother when I next ring. As for names – I have no idea.

Gunther.

It didn't take Rose long to allocate new names to the hens: Ingrid, Esther and, of course, Frieda, collectively known as the girlies. And, to her amazement, she had two fresh eggs for breakfast.

34.

Nellie and Rose had a relatively quiet few days. She'd been too exhausted to try and reconnect with any of her visions; they were definitely taking their toll and she'd needed a rest. She'd filled her time baking for the café and strolling with Nellie through the countryside, but Friday evening soon came around. Not long after Alan had left, Shona and Freya arrived together along with Meg. Nellie was getting used to the growing menagerie around her and looked forward to Freya's visits. As always, Shona took charge, decanting her tools of the trade under the elm tree at the bottom of the back garden while the hens looked on with interest.

"What's that for?" Rose asked, when Shona lifted what looked like a wooden chopping board out of the bottom of the basket.

"It's a Ouija board."

Rose stared open mouthed; she'd read about them but never actually seen one before. It looked innocent enough, she thought, but she knew they could be dangerous in the wrong hands.

"I hope you know what you're doing!"

Shona and Freya shared a look that Rose didn't like. She was even more perplexed when Shona went back to her car and returned with a metal cauldron.

"And what's that for?"

Taking her to one side, Freya put her hand on Rose's shoulder. "For the fire."

"But I thought we'd agreed – no more fires."

"We agreed no more fires inside. Besides, it's contained," Shona shouted back.

Rose sighed, hoping it would stay that way.

The next thing to appear was the old rocking chair. It was heavy but, somehow, Freya managed to drag it outside then plonked herself into it. "There, I think we're ready."

The three women sat around the small fire, under the elm tree, with Nellie and Meg at their sides. Shona carefully arranged the Ouija board on the table between them and began to speak.

"This evening, we welcome back the old spirits of this land. If you are with us, please make your presence known."

A cold breeze rustled the leaves in the tree above their heads and the flames died down.

"Are you here William?"

Freya was the first to move. Leaning forward, she gestured to the others then placed her hands on the planchette. "William, is that you?"

Without hesitation, the planchette moved up the board to NO. Freya sagged; she needed to speak to William.

"Who is this, if not William?"

Again, the planchette moved, this time down and began to slide across the board: A N N E.

Freya looked up and beamed. This was what she'd been waiting for. A shiver ran down Rose's spine; she didn't like this way of communicating at all. She much preferred visions; they were simpler. You knew where you were with visions, she thought. But Freya was invested; her concentration was palpable.

"Welcome Anne. What do you want to tell us today?"

Once more, with a mind of its own, the planchette travelled across the surface of the board and Freya read the letters out loud. "F A M I L Y. Family. Whose family Anne?"

"M I N E. Mine. Do you mean you, Anne?"

"Y E S. Yes. Your family?"

"Y E S. Yes." Freya looked at her companions, but

neither spoke. Shona nodded, urging her on.

"Who is family, Anne?"

"Y O U. You. Who, Anne? Do you mean me, Freya?"

"Y E S. Yes."

Startled by a sudden movement behind her, Rose jumped up. At the same time, the flames in the cauldron leapt high into the air, sending a spray of sparks skywards. Rose gasped when she turned and came face to face with Alan.

She put her hand to her mouth. "W, what are you doing here?"

"I do happen to live here, and I was about to ask you three the same question."

A flash high above caused them all to look up. To Rose's horror, she saw that some of the leaves in the elm tree had caught fire. A stiff breeze circled them, fanning the flames, causing the fire to spread higher into the branches. Rose was now frozen to the spot, but Alan already had the hosepipe attached to the outside tap and was quickly directing water towards the tree.

"The pressure isn't high enough - Rose get the jet washer out of the shed and plug it in!"

Professional mode swiftly kicked in, and Rose had it all set up in minutes. Alan attached the hose and soon had water spraying high into the tree's canopy. Before too long, the fire was extinguished and the four of them stood looking dazed, soaking wet and covered in charred leaves in the back garden.

Rose broke the silence. "Where're Nellie and Meg?"

Alan pointed and the three women turned to see the two pets peering out of the patio window.

"Right, let's get cleaned up. I'll pour some wine and perhaps you could explain what you were doing setting fire to our garden, Rose?"

Speechless, Rose stared at her husband. "But ... but, you're supposed to be at a rally."

"It got cancelled at the last minute, something to do with the venue. Just as well really, or I might not have had a home to return to!"

It took Rose almost two hours to make her confession and recount the whole story of her journey into witchcraft. Surprisingly, Alan was all ears at first, but, as Rose had predicted, when the tale got stranger, he struggled to take her seriously. With back up from Freya and Shona, his scepticism eased a little and was followed by relief.

"Now do you believe me?"

He walked over to his wife. "I'm not so sure Rose, it sounds a little crazy. I think I'd need to see some evidence." Bending down, he held her hand and pulled her out of the chair, hugging her before placing a passionate kiss on her lips. "It sure beats the reasons I'd conjured up as to why you were acting secretively though."

Trying hard to hide her embarrassment at having kissed Alan in front of her friends, she stuttered, "W, what do you mean?"

Alan was grinning like a Cheshire cat and kissed his wife once more. "I thought you were having an affair."

"What? Me, having an affair – it's you that's having an affair!"

Alan stepped back. "What do you mean?"

"Well, you're away so many weekends, I thought you had a mistress, someone from the motorsport club perhaps."

Smiling, he took Rose's hand once more. "Do you think I would have turned back tonight when the rally was cancelled if I'd got another woman? It's you, Rose, only you that I love."

A short while later, all four of them were laughing at the misunderstanding. Shona had drunk too much wine to drive back home, so she and Freya had to stay the night.

It was just turned midnight when Alan needed a drink of water; the wine had left his mouth feeling a little parched. Mindful not to wake his guests, he crept down the corridor but stopped when he saw the study door open. Peeping inside he was surprised to see Freya wearing a strange garment like the one he'd seen Rose wearing once before. She was sitting in the rocking chair, seemingly talking to herself.

"Family, but what do you mean?" he heard her say.

She appeared frustrated and he was about to walk away when, out of the corner of his eye, he saw a pile of papers on the desk rise into the air and then settle back down. Shocked, he stared in disbelief. What had just happened? How was it possible? Confused, he shook his head. Perhaps he'd imagined it; it had been a strange evening after all! Rooted to the spot, he peered further into the room. A few seconds later, the photograph of Amy and Vicky as babies toppled over on the shelf. Was he seeing things or was his home really haunted by the spirits of the past?

Suddenly, Freya looked up and saw him standing in the hall. Sighing, she beckoned him in.

"What on earth just happened? This is insane! Tell me you saw it too!"

"Yes, it's Anne again. This has happened before, but I don't know the significance of the moving papers, or the photo of the girls. It's something to do with family."

Alan nodded with wide eyes, still unsure if he believed

in witchcraft. "I actually saw that. This is madness!" Taking a deep breath, he tried to relax. Clearly this wasn't Freya's fault. "W, what are those papers?"

Freya picked them up. "Notes that Rose made when she was searching the ancestry website to find out who William was. His initials are carved under this rocking chair."

"Yes, I've seen them - and the box and ring." He scratched his head wondering how he could help. "Anyway, there's nothing we can do now. You go back to bed, Freya; try and get some rest. We'll talk in the morning."

He waited until Freya had closed the door of the guest room before entering the study. They really needed to get to the bottom of this. But what could he do?

The three women were having breakfast when Alan appeared. Rose looked up from her cereal. "Ah, there you are, I wondered where you were when I woke up this morning. Thought you might have gone for a walk."

"No, just had a few emails to sort out."

What he didn't confess to the chatting trio was what he'd really been doing most of the night; he'd been sitting in the study. First of all, he'd meticulously gone through the details Rose had managed to find, then he'd trawled through all of the parish records and finally searched every census. It had been extremely tedious work, but, having witnessed the strange events in the very same room earlier, he'd felt compelled to try and help – to solve the mystery - not only for the sake of the three women but for the safety of his wife and home. He couldn't have Rose involved in dangerous pursuits, and if that meant getting on board and helping then that was a small price to pay for her safety. His darling Rose. She meant everything to him. He couldn't believe that she'd thought he was having an affair, and he'd thought she was too. The whole situation had got truly out of hand.

"Communicate," he whispered to himself, "we need to communicate more."

"Pardon?" Rose looked at Alan and thought he looked to have dark circles round his eyes.

"Oh, nothing, Love. I was just deciding what to have for breakfast."

Once Shona and Freya had said their goodbyes, Rose went out into the back garden. "The tree looks better than I'd imagined."

"Yes," Alan agreed, "it's only burnt off some of the dry leaves. They'll regrow in the spring. It could have been much worse."

The pair sat on the patio and Rose turned to her husband. "I'm so sorry for this," she gestured towards the tree, "and everything - for doubting you and..."

Alan silenced his wife with a kiss. "I'm sorry too. We need to learn to communicate more - and I've decided to participate in fewer events. We need to do more things together." Rose leaned her head on his shoulder and relaxed. "There's something else I need to show you too."

Reaching into his pocket, Alan produced a neatly folded piece of A4 paper which he handed to his wife.

"What is it?"

"Have a look."

Unfolding the paper, Rose scanned over its contents. "It's a family tree."

"Take a closer look."

After finding her glasses, Rose stared in disbelief. "Wow! When did you do this... how... but... why, why didn't you show us this at breakfast?"

"I don't know Freya very well; it would be better coming from you."

Rose threw her arms around her husband's neck and squeezed the life out of him. "Thank you! Thank you so much. This is unbelievable. I need to ring her now."

Alan took hold of Rose's hand. "Don't, Love, not now. Let's have a quiet weekend alone, getting to know each other again. I don't want to lose you – ever."

On Monday morning, after kissing his wife, Alan climbed into his car. "I can't remember the last time I enjoyed myself so much. Go and tell Freya your news." He blew her a kiss through the car window then stopped and leaned his head out. "And remember – no more fires."

Smiling, Rose nodded and waved then went back inside to retrieve the family tree that Alan had spent all of Friday night compiling. She was so proud of him. She knew this was going to blow Freya's mind. Now she understood what Anne had been trying to tell her.

"Good morning, I wasn't expecting you. Have you had a good weekend?" Freya wiggled her eyebrows and Rose blushed. "What have you got there?"

"I think you need to make a pot of strong coffee before I show you this."

Frowning, Freya put the kettle on, feeling a little unnerved. "What's wrong?"

"Nothing, nothing at all." And, for once, Rose felt that all was well in her little world.

"Okay, hand it over – whatever it is."

Hesitating, Rose passed the sheet of paper to her friend, knowing this might well open up a can of worms for her.

Carefully, Freya unfolded the document and glanced

over it. "It's a family tree."

"Yes, but look more closely."

After a few minutes, Freya held her hand to her mouth and let out a sob. "It's ... it's me." Her head snapped up and her piercing emerald green eyes glistened with tears. "I'm William and Anne's great, great, great granddaughter."

Rose was at her side with her arm around her shoulder. "So it would appear."

Freya rested her head on Rose and cried. For the first time in her life, she really felt as though she truly belonged. She'd been abandoned into the care system by her mother and had never known a loving family. She'd endured years of hardship and abuse, been shunned by many. Since she'd escaped her abusive husband, many years ago, she'd never been able to trust again. Not until now. Not until she'd met Shona and Rose. And now Alan – he was added to her short list of friends, genuine friends.

"I almost feel as though I'm related to you," Freya whispered.

"Me too. We're honorary sisters."

"I'll drink to that!"

Freya picked her mug up and drained the last of her coffee and let her eyes stray to the document in front of her. Gently, she traced a finger over the writing as the words sank in.

William had been born in Ireland and came over in the great potato famine. He'd married Anne in 1860 then Lavinia was born in 1862. Sadly, Anne had died but Lavinia had survived.

Lavinia had married in 1882 and she herself had produced a daughter called Ethel in 1887.

Ethel went on to have a son called Ben, then Ben's wife, Hannah had borne a daughter called Edie in 1948. Edie was Freya's mother.

Rose held tight onto her friend's hand while they sat in silence, taking the information in. She was the first to speak. "I feel as though my little cottage should belong to you, not me."

Freya looked up at her friend. "Nope, they were only tenants, and you bought it. It definitely belongs to you and Alan, and I can't think of anyone I'd prefer to be the custodian of my great, great, great grandparents' home."

"The rocking chair; I'll get Alan to bring it over for you."

Wiping the tears from her stained face, Freya sagged. "Nope again, it belongs with the cottage, and I think we should call it 'the witch's chair'." Beaming, Rose hugged her friend even tighter, squeezing Freya until she was breathless. When she released her Freya continued, "I'll be happy just to come over and sit in it once in a while."

"You're welcome anytime, you know that. Now, close your eyes."

Rose took a small wooden box out of her bag and retrieved the precious object from within. It was the ring, Anne's wedding ring. Rose knew it would be too small to fit on Freya's fingers, so she'd threaded it onto a plain gold chain. Leaning over she fastened the chain around Freya's neck.

Freya shuddered; it felt as though the metal was white hot against her skin. Reaching up, she held the ring away from her neck. A tingling feeling travelled through her veins to every part of her soul. Family. There was nothing more precious than family.

"Are you sure?" she gasped. "It's your property."

Nodding, Rose felt tears prickling the corner of her eyes. "I've never been surer. But there's more."

"I'm not sure I can take anything else in."

Once more, Rose dipped into her bag and held out the bowl of the small clay pipe that had been dug out of the front garden, "This must have belonged to William; it came from Ireland too." Freya's green eyes shone even brighter as she took hold of the object."

"I'll treasure this forever. Thank you." Freya sat back

and sighed; she couldn't hide from the past any longer. "I suppose you want to hear my story now? How I stumbled through life as an orphan."

Hugging her best friend tight, she whispered into her ear, "Only when you feel ready to tell me."

36.

"How did that go, Love?" Alan asked when he got home.

"Amazing. It took her a while for it to sink in, as it did with us, then she was over the moon."

After dinner, Alan snuggled on the sofa next to his beautiful wife – a witch. Who would have thought it? But all that mattered to him now was that they were here together, his special Rose. She was clever, compassionate and funny, the perfect wife and mother. How would he have ever managed without her?

Grazing the back of her hand with his lips, he gazed into her eyes. "Well, that was exciting. What will you do to fill your days now, Love? It might feel like a bit of an anti-climax."

Rose didn't get chance to think about Alan's question; her mobile phone was ringing. It was a number she didn't recognise, so she put it onto speakerphone so that Alan could hear.

"Hello."

"Hi Rose, it's Amelia, forensic psychology department. Sorry to bother you so late, but a cold case has just presented itself in your area and I was hoping you might be able to help."

"Oh, hi Amelia, I, er, I don't know what to say."

"Sleep on it and ring me back tomorrow."

Laughter lines crinkled around Alan's eyes. "Oh Rose, whatever will you discover next?"

THE END

THE WORLD BEYOND

Chapter One

Hungry for oxygen, Rose spluttered and sat bolt upright in bed.

"What is it Rose? Are you okay?" Filled with concern,

Alan was immediately at his wife's side, pressing a glass of cold water into her hand. Comforted by his presence her erratic breathing gradually steadied while he stroked her damp hair across her forehead. Reassured, he continued. "Another vision?"

"Yes."

"What was it this time?"

Sagging into his embrace she shrugged and failed to respond.

"You know love – if it's too much you don't have to do this."

Again, she failed to supply him with an explanation, so he squeezed her hand tight.

"I ... I want to Alan. I might as well put my abilities to good use." Turning away she stood up and stared out of the window, "Sometimes though, it feels more like a curse than a blessing."

"It's still early; come back to bed for an hour."

"No, I need to get it down on paper then send it to Amelia; it might be relevant."

Hi Amelia,

Don't know if this helps, but I've just had another brief

vision. I saw a slim, young woman, from behind, walking along a path next to a river. She was wearing skinny jeans and a navy-blue hoodie which I'm sure had white writing on it. Her mouse brown hair was secured high on her head in a ponytail. She stepped under an arched bridge into darkness. Then I woke up. Oh yes – one more thing, she had a white carrier bag in her left hand. It looked heavy.

Sorry, it's not much to go on.

Rose.

The following morning, Rose found herself in the city. She detested the noise and commotion, but she was thankful that Alan had updated her satnav – it was very thoughtful of him, she reflected. At last, she'd managed to park her small car near the office. Wearing her new black trouser suit and crisp white blouse Rose anxiously made her way inside. She'd received a text from Amelia earlier asking her to come in as soon as possible. Apparently, it was urgent.

"Good morning Rose, thanks for coming at such short notice." Amelia gestured towards a chair in the compact meeting room. "This is DCI Tom Jarrod."

Feeling a little anxious, Rose tried to smile at the young man sat at the table with a laptop open in front of him. Was she old enough to be his mother she wondered?

"Good morning, nice to meet you Rose. Do sit down."

Still uneasy, Rose sat at the table next to Amelia wondering how she should address DCI Jarrod. Sensing the tension in the room, Amelia broke the silence. "Tom is from CID."

Rose, her mouth parched, took a while to form a coherent sentence. Eventually, she turned to Amelia. "Is this about the vision I had? Sorry it was rather vague."

Amelia nodded; she didn't want to alarm Rose; it was still early days. They'd only been working together for a couple of weeks, but this was bizarre. Extremely bizarre. She'd worked with mediums before but never come across anything quite like it and didn't know where to begin.

After clearing his throat, Tom spoke. "Rose, the young girl in your vision, did you know her? Had you ever seen her before?"

"No Sir, but I never actually saw her face; she was walking away with her back to me."

"Please call me Tom." He leaned forward and steepled his manicured fingers under his chin, wondering how to continue. He felt way out of his comfort zone. This was crazy, he couldn't believe he was actually doing this - but he knew he had to get it right this time or the shit would really hit the fan. "So Rose, could you tell me about the location? By a river you said."

"Yes, that's correct, she was walking alongside a river then disappeared from view underneath an arched bridge. I think it was made out of stone – it looked old."

"Was it somewhere you'd been before?"

Concentrating hard, Rose tried to remember the scene. "Erm, no Sir, erm, Tom. It didn't look familiar. Do you think it's relevant?"

"Yes, it's relevant, Rose." He sighed, then looked over to his colleague for support.

Taking over, Amelia turned to face her. "Rose, early this morning a cyclist on his way to work discovered the body of a young woman under a bridge floating in the Huddersfield narrow canal."

Rose's head snapped up and she stared wide eyed at Tom who was now holding a sheet of card. He turned it over. Startled, she held her hand to her mouth. It was an image of a young woman laid out on a slab.

"Sorry. Didn't mean to alarm you; it can be distressing." Leaning forward he slid the photo across the table. "Is this the same woman, Rose?"

Amelia stood and pressed her hand on Rose's shoulder. "Take your time, Rose. I'll get us some coffee."

Unable to speak, Rose picked up the photo. She wasn't easily shocked – she'd seen many dead bodies in her professional life as a nurse - but never a murder victim.

Concentrating, she studied the image for a while. A gaping wound above the left eye revealed soft tissue billowing out with congealed blood matting her brown hair. Was this the cause of death? Rose cleared her throat. "How did she die?"

"We haven't established cause of death yet. Do you recognise her, Rose?" The door to the small room opened and Amelia returned with three coffees, momentarily distracting her. "Rose?"

"Sorry, I, er, I don't recognise the woman. As I said, I only saw her from behind, but the clothes look the same." Rose ran her hand through her hair and removed her glasses. "Was there any writing on the back of the hoodie?"

Tom leaned in and handed her another photo, this time an image containing only the clothes that the woman had been wearing. On the back of the navy-blue hoodie, it read UNIVERSITY OF HUDDERSFIELD in bold white letters. Rose closed her eyes. What was she doing here? Why was she putting herself through this? Perhaps Alan was right. She shouldn't be doing this.

"Rose, does it look familiar?" he snapped, while glancing at his phone as it pinged with an incoming message.

"Yes. Yes, it does. Was she a student?"

"No, we've spoken to the university. She wasn't a

student there." Drawing his well-groomed, brown eyebrows into a scowl, he leaned back on the uncomfortable chair. "So, just to be sure, you think this could be the same young woman you saw in your vision - the vision you had twenty-four hours before her death?"

"Yes, it's possible. The clothes appear to match."

Gathering the photos together, he sighed, "And just so we can rule you out of our investigation, Rose, can you tell me of your whereabouts last night?"

ABOUT THE AUTHOR

Emma Sharp is the author of the popular Chateau Trilogy, comprising of: The Letter, Sweet Pea and Secrets and Surprises.

Emma, a former nurse was born and raised in Yorkshire. She has two grown up daughters, a grand-daughter and a much-loved Cavapoo, Molly. She loves to travel and finds that she writes her best work when she's at her caravan amidst the stunning scenery of the Yorkshire Dales.

She has also appeared on local radio reading her short stories and is a member of a writing group, who meet regularly to review and appraise each other's work.

I hope you enjoy reading her novels.

Printed in Great Britain
by Amazon